**LAURAINE SNELLING'S**

novels appear regularly on the CBA bestseller
list, and there are more than two million copies
of her books in print. She and her husband have
two grown sons and make their home in California.

**LENORA WORTH**

is the award-winning author of over sixteen
Love Inspired romances and two novels for
Steeple Hill. She lives in Shreveport, Louisiana,
and is married and the mother of two.

# LAURAINE SNELLING
## LENORA WORTH

# ONCE UPON A CHRISTMAS

Steeple Hill®

Published by Steeple Hill Books™

STEEPLE HILL BOOKS

Steeple
Hill®

ISBN-13:  978-0-373-78549-0
ISBN-10:     0-373-78549-6

ONCE UPON A CHRISTMAS

Copyright © 2006 by Harlequin Books S.A.

The publisher acknowledges the copyright holders
of the individual works as follows:

THE MOST WONDERFUL TIME OF THE YEAR
Copyright © 2005 by Lauraine Snelling

'TWAS THE WEEK BEFORE CHRISTMAS
Copyright © 2005 by Lenora H. Nazworth

www.SteepleHill.com

**Printed in U.S.A.**

# CONTENTS

THE MOST WONDERFUL TIME        9
   OF THE YEAR
Lauraine Snelling

'TWAS THE WEEK BEFORE       155
   CHRISTMAS
Lenora Worth

# THE MOST WONDERFUL TIME OF THE YEAR

## Lauraine Snelling

❧ ❧ ❧

Dedicated to the Basset Rescue Connection
and those who rescue dogs of all breeds

Special thanks to Chewy, Woofer and Missy—
my basset inspirations

# CHAPTER ONE

"I feel as creative as a blob of clay and tomorrow I turn the big three-oh."

Harley looked up at her, adoration in his sad, basset eyes, his tail beating the finish off the office chair legs.

"Yeah, I know. You want to go for a walk. But Harley, Christmas is coming and I'm not anywhere near to ready. Not even begun, if truth be told. Now I know I'm never really ready for Christmas but—this time I'm beyond hope." Blythe Stensrude glanced at the harbinger of despair again. Calendars should be banned from polite society. "Think I'll skip Christmas this year, right along with my birthday." Leaning down from her office chair, she cupped his furry face in her hands and looked deeply into his dark brown eyes. "Another Christmas single. I thought for sure I'd be married by now." *I once dreamed of children but not anymore.* She slammed the door on that near-tragic memory without peeking through.

A sigh stopped further confidences for a moment,

while pictures of former suitors, or at least daters, flipped Rolodex-fashion through her mind. Thomas, college years, earring, musician. Boris, internship, Austrian, intriguing, bad breath. Henderson, first job, ladder climber, married her best friend. Sanchez, second job, wanted big family, huh-uh, not in this lifetime. Jones, real possibility, married, the jerk. And her rather unusual, but necessary requirement, no desire for fatherhood.

Harley kissed the tip of her nose with a lightning tongue.

Blythe sighed again. None. Nada. "From now on, no more blind dates, no more 'come for dinner' and there's an extra man there, just for me. I'll just tell those nosey noses, yes, I have a man in my life. His name is Harley."

Hearing his name, Harley planted both front paws on her knees and, tail wagging, whined again, then swiped her chin with a black-spotted pink tongue.

She hugged him close and got her ear cleaned, for her trouble.

Harley whimpered again and dropped to the floor. He headed toward the door, giving her an imploring glance over his shoulder.

"Oh, all right." Blythe snapped the blue nylon leash to the dog's collar. "And the final thing, I'm going to learn to be content with you as the man in my life. God seems to have forgotten that dream of mine, in spite of a multitude of reminders."

With the leash in place, Harley headed for the door. One either followed or spent hours teaching the dog manners, an exercise which Blythe had been promising herself to do.

"You have to let me get my coat, you silly thing." She dropped the leash and stood on her end while retrieving her purple, fleece-lined jacket. The wind in Martinez, California, could carry a real bite down at the marina park where she loved to walk and Harley loved to nose for the smells, always anticipating the rabbit he might catch one day.

Key in her teeth to lock the dead bolt, she opened the front door. Harley made a dive for the outside, just as the phone rang. Answer it. No, let the machine pick it up.

The sigh came from her toes. "Get back in here, you big lug." She hauled back on the leash, dragging the nail-scrabbling dog back in the house. The door slammed closed and she dove for the phone, getting it just as the answering machine clicked in.

"Blythe's Graphics. Let me put pictures to your words. I'm either…"

"I'm here, don't hang up, the message will be over in a moment." *Why haven't I learned how to turn off the message? Why do I let some of this stuff…?* "Hello, yes this is Blythe, how may I help you?"

"Good morning, Blythe, Brad Cummings here, wondering how the artwork for my project is coming? Are we on schedule?"

Blythe groaned inside but kept a smile on her face, having learned how important a smile is to the tone of voice on the phone, or anywhere for that matter. "Barring any natural disasters, I should be finished tomorrow night, just as we agreed." *Now why did I say that?* But she knew why. She loved this man's laugh, which he did as if programmed. The deep baritone chuckle came across the wires as if he were right beside her. The only problem with this man? He was happily married with three children, all of whom sang in the youth choirs at church.

"Give me a call, then, and I'll be by to pick up the package. I'll stop on my way home. Save you a trip. Bye."

Blythe set the phone back in the stand. That project would be done even if she never slept tonight.

Sometimes becoming successful led to other problems, like too much of a good thing. A good thing, meaning work of course. As a graphic artist, she was making a name for herself. But how was she to keep the quality up to her standards when she had so much to do? And such tight deadlines. She could hear her mother plain as the dog whining at her feet. "Sometimes you have to learn to say no." Sometimes…yeah, well, she'd have to practice that— in her spare time.

"I'm coming, Harley, but this is going to have to be one quick walk."

She locked the front door of her semirestored Victorian cottage and pulled on her turquoise gloves as Harley, russet-colored ears dragging the ground, and nose leading the way, turned left at the open gate of the picket fence. He knew the shortest way to the marina as well as she did so she only chose an alternate route if she didn't mind an argument.

Blythe lifted her face to catch the intermittent sun rays as clouds played tag with the wind. After two days of fog and rain, which left her feeling out of sorts, the sun felt like a gift she almost didn't open. Not that she was a sun worshipper, but waking to sunshine in the morning always set her day on the right track.

She groaned when her dog stopped to investigate something really important, though only he could discern what creature had passed that way.

"Harley, you could at least warn me." And you could pay, *should* pay, better attention. There was that voice, the one she frequently wanted to strangle.

His tail wagged, but his broad black nose never left the ground. When he ran out of scent, he raised his head, grinned at her and trotted out again, his snowshoe feet slapping the sidewalk.

"Top of the mornin' to ye." June Simmons, who lived on the next block, finished filling one of her twenty bird feeders and met them at her gate.

"And to you. New part?"

"I'm needin' to be authentic Irish in a week."

"Good for you, you'll make it. Which theater?"

"The Willows. Look at ye, lass, life must be goin' yer way. Faith and begorra, ye've been a yellow-headed lassie for six months an' more."

"Really? Humph." Blythe pulled at the ends of the shag cut. "It's needin' cuttin', that's what it is."

June bent down and rubbed Harley's ears, then removed the dog biscuit from her pocket and asked, "Ye bein' hungry, Harley, dear?"

Harley yipped but when she shook her head, gave in and barked in basso profundo, true hound fashion.

"Ah, that's more like it." June handed him the treat she

double baked herself. "Ye better be watchin' for the wee folk down at the park. Heard tell there's been sightings."

"If they hide in rabbit holes, Harley is sure to find one." Leaving June laughing, the two walked on down the hill, Harley now tugging on the leash.

They crossed the railroad tracks to enter the park at the west end. With the tide out, the wind blew the rank odor of mudflats their way. The freeway bridge arched over the Sacramento River from Martinez to Benicia. While most of the shipping consisted of oil tankers, pleasure boats, ships bringing grain from the upper rivers and container ships also plied the river waters. The two rivers converged upriver a few miles and flowed through the Carquinez Straits into the San Francisco Bay. Since the wind was from the west, she couldn't smell the refineries for a change. Even the pungent mudflats were preferable to the refineries.

Harley stuck his nose in a hole dug into the low grassy bank.

This did not promise to be a fast walk at all; he was in a real investigative mood.

"Sorry, Harley, come." She tugged on the leash. He wagged his tail. Moving a busy basset was like dragging a watersoaked log—through the mud. "Harley! I have tons of work to do, so it's walk or go home. Take your pick."

A rabbit darted out of the other end of the hole. From standing still to dead run in one bound, his back feet threw mud and grass as he dug for traction. Harley hit the end of the leash.

Blythe dug in her heels, but her purple boots could get no footing. "Harley!"

# CHAPTER TWO

Thane Davidson stared at the dog at his feet. If relaxed needed a picture, a sleeping basset fit. Especially Matty, his three-year-old fawn-and-white female, the only real steady female in his life at the moment. She had "relax" down to a science.

"I asked if you wanted to go for a walk. I'm going and if you get up, you'll get to *go,* too." He put the emphasis on the word go. "I know this is outside of your schedule but…"

She opened both eyes, wagged the white tip of her tail and with a groan and a prolonged stretch, got to her feet. Not that she could get very far up. While bassets are big-dog size in the body, in the leg department, they got woefully shortchanged.

He half smiled at the look of long suffering she sent his way. "Don't bother, I don't do guilt." When he reached down and stroked her head and long ears, he marveled, as always, at how soft she was. Adoration was his for the petting, so he continued. Everyone needed to be adored at one time or another.

He smoothed down her long back and scratched her favorite spot, between her front shoulder blades, then rubbed along her spine.

"That's all. We need to hit the street before the phone rings again." He headed for the closet for his anorak and her leash. As soon as they were both dressed, they left the house, he with his cell phone in his pocket after a brief tussle with "take it along" or "leave it home." But since he was on call 24/7 as a troubleshooter for several computer software giants, he had learned never to be out of touch. Even though he sometimes felt like he was on a tighter leash than his dog.

He locked the condo door and, leash in hand, strolled toward the elevator. The doors on either side of his door sported holiday wreaths, one including an angel. Wasn't it a bit early for such decorations? Thane punched the elevator button with a little more force than necessary. Health wise he should take the stairs but Matty hated stairs, especially four flights. He couldn't say he blamed her—dragging your belly over all those ridges would aggravate anyone. He stopped just outside the entry to adjust his collar.

"Hey, Mister Davidson, you walking your own dog?"

Did the kid from 3A ever do anything but ride his bike in front of the building?

"Looks that way."

"Where's Josie?"

"I don't know." *I'm not Josie's keeper, she just walks*

*my dog when I'm not home.* Which is most of the time. During the day, at least. Since his clients were located in the Bay area, he did manage to sleep at home—usually.

"She's not sick or anything?"

"Not to my knowledge."

"You going to pay her anyway? She needs the money." The boy stopped his bike, facing into the curb.

Thane swallowed a growl when Matty pulled on the leash, anxious to greet the boy on the bike. Had this kid no manners at all, telling him how to run his life?

"And that's your business?"

The red-headed charmer shrugged and leaned down to scratch Matty behind the ears. He knew her favorite places, as evidenced by the wriggling joy and her happy yips.

"No, I s'pose not." He looked up again, blue eyes serious. "But Josie needs someone to look out for her."

*Lord, save me. I cannot be the savior for all young women.* Was Josie a druggie like LynnEllen, his younger and only sister? "If Josie is doing drugs, I'll have no part of her."

"Nah, she don't do drugs." The look he sent Thane carried a trainload of disdain. He shook his head and with a jerk of the handlebars, spun his bike and pedaled away. "Josie's real good with Matty." The words floated back over his shoulder. "You're lucky. Maybe you could give her a big Christmas present."

"Put down by a kid. Matty, what's this world coming to?" What was he coming to? He'd stayed to listen. Used up five minutes of his precious time. All over the dog walker. Of course Josie took Matty to the vet's when needed, the groomer on schedule and dog-sat when he was forced to be gone overnight. She seemed to have a solid clientele. Could one make a living at such a precarious business? Had she complained that he didn't pay her enough?

"I'll ask her if she should increase her rates."

Matty glanced back over her shoulder, then, head and tail high, trotted toward the marina, about half a mile away. While sometimes they drove, when the weather was decent they walked. And at times even jogged.

Today Thane didn't feel like jogging. He glanced upward. Why if the sun was shining did he feel like the heaviest of clouds surrounded him, squashing him down like a bug under someone's heel?

What he needed was a five-mile run. But Matty couldn't run that far, so it was down to the marina for an outing and then he'd take the car out to drive to Briones Park and a good long run. That would put him back in a normal mood.

His cell phone chimed, a businesslike ring, not one of the silly songs some users subscribed to. He punched the green bar. "Davidson."

"Thane." Her voice had more energy than he'd heard in it for a long time.

"Linnie." For some reason he used the childhood name for his sister, LynnEllen. His sister who'd gotten hooked on drugs in college and thrown her life away. That was bad enough, but she now had a three-year-old daughter whose life was also in jeopardy.

"Merry Christmas, brother mine."

"Not yet." He slowed to a walk, the phone at his ear as they crossed Alhambra Avenue. The picket fence in front of them wore garlands of cedar and big red bows. Matching pots of red cyclamen brightened the front porch.

"Don't go all humbug on me." Her voice lost its forced cheer. "I'm clean and sober, thanks to you and this latest rehab, and I want us to spend Christmas as a family."

"Linnie, I…"

"I know, I know. I've blown the last years, but this time is different."

That's what you always say and then… For one brief moment he saw the two of them, giggling outside the arch to the living room where the tree waited in all its glory, that interminable Christmas morning wait for their parents to join them. But in more recent years—drunk was bad enough, but what about stoned? *The time you passed out, taking the tree down with you. The year I bailed you out of jail, big as a house with Amie.* He felt like cramming the phone back in his pocket or dumping it in the trash receptacle he'd just passed.

"I have an apartment now and furniture even."

Amazing what you can do with your allowance when you don't drink or snort it. They both received monthly dividends from the trust fund left from their parents' insurance and estate. He'd set it up so she could get only a monthly allowance, never access to the principle. His share he put in a trust fund for Amie, without LynnEllen's knowledge.

"It's really important that you come. Amie is old enough to know she has a real family."

He could tell she was fighting tears.

"Please?"

"Look, you know I'm on call 24/7. If something comes up…"

"Thane, you are the *head* of your company. You can do what you want, there are others who can fill in for one day. Besides, everything closes down for Christmas anyway." Her voice had regained its strength.

*Perhaps, just maybe, please, God, this time let it work.*

"I'm doing AA. And I've found a church that welcomes me as I am. I just want you to rejoice with me, big brother."

Thane blew out a cheek-puffing breath, wanting to congratulate her even as he doubted a positive outcome. "All right. I'll fly down on the morning of the twenty-fourth."

"Amie's preschool program is the morning of the twenty-third. I hoped you could come for that, too."

A cloud passed over the sun.

"I'll see." His sister had used Amie as a pawn before. He wondered what was going on this time.

"Good. Thank you, Thane. You won't regret this."

I pray to God not. "Bye." He snapped the phone shut and dropped it back in his pocket.

What had he gotten himself into now?

The soles of his shoes slammed against the concrete as he picked up the pace again. Why had he agreed? Why had he not given her more approval? She needed him, he was the only family she had left. But he'd sworn to wash his hands of her. No more enabling.

Matty yipped and when he turned he saw her tongue hanging out and her ribs pumping like the proverbial bellows. Had he been dragging her along...what, two blocks, three?

He stopped and knelt in front of her. "I'm sorry, girl. You okay?"

She collapsed at his feet, her dark eyes forgiving him while she fought to catch her breath.

What kind of a jerk are you? Not paying attention to your dog even? You ought to be turned over to the Society for Prevention of Cruelty to Animals.

*What about cruelty to relatives?* The thought hissed its way through his mental scolding.

He clamped his teeth, eyes narrowed. Tough love, that's what he'd been forced to resort to. He refused to be an enabler any longer. LynnEllen had to take responsibility for her own actions. That's what the counselor had told them both.

He knew the odds of breaking crack addiction. Slim to none. He'd long since stopped hoping. He stroked Matty, something that always calmed him, the soft fur beneath his fingertips, her heart no longer slamming against her ribs.

"Perhaps we better just head on home."

She raised her head and licked his wrist, feather soft, then pushed herself to her feet and pointed her nose toward the marina, sniffing the air as if they were already there.

"Okay, I get the point. But we'll take it easy, all right?"

Her tail dusted the sidewalk.

A couple minutes later they crossed the new pedestrian bridge over the railroad tracks by the new Amtrak passenger station and followed the trail down toward the marina. Once the area had been a landfill, and oldsters told of coming down there to shoot rats. Now Oak and other trees shaded thick grass where families gathered for picnics, Frisbee tosses, and sometimes set up volleyball nets. On the other side of the main road down to the boating launch a bocce ball court drew devoted fans, further east were softball and soccer fields and even a riding arena where horse shows drew big crowds. But the path Thane traveled wound its way down to the duck pond, and the new pier which shadowed the decaying wharf. At the pond he took the trail that ambled west through the wetlands, Matty trotting ladylike beside him. They crossed the arched bridge over a creek, stopping at the top to look out across the mudflats. A gray heron stood sentinel on the steep banks of the creek. White egrets patrolled the mudflats, along with squawking gulls and dabbling dowitchers.

A dog barked.

Matty hit the dirt trail leading off to the west with three bounds, ripping the lead from his hand.

"Matty! Stop! Stay!" He might well have been ordering the wind.

# CHAPTER THREE

Only in cartoons did the person on the end of a dog leash go airborne, feet straight out from a horizontal body. Or at least that's what Blythe assumed, until she found herself in a similar state.

"Harley! Stop!" She yelped as she was ploughed through scrub brush. "Harley! Sit! Sit, Harley!" Her knees bumped against a hillock of sea grass and her hand automatically released the lead so she could catch her fall.

"Oomph! Ouch. Harley, when I catch you… Harley, come!" She slammed a gloved palm against the ground and pushed herself to her feet. "That dog. Anyone who owns a basset needs her head examined. Harley!"

She stared around the brushy terrain that alternated with tall grasses, sneaky mud pits and swamp. She heard his deep woof from off to her right, and it escalated to a frenzy of higher pitched barks. Another dog answered.

At the same time a deep human voice yelled, "Matty!"

No need to worry about Harley. He'd found his best

friend. But the voice calling the dog was definitely not Josie. She was an alto at the lowest, not deep baritone or high bass.

Blythe brushed the detritus of her fall from the front of her jacket, frowned at the mud on one jeans-clad knee and jogged toward the reunion. She could hear the two dogs whining and yipping their delight.

She'd heard that dogs often grew to look like their owners, or vice versa, but not in this case. The man walking toward her was a dead ringer for a younger Sam Elliott. Same dark hair, bushy brows over eyes that right now were snapping with fury. Only the luxuriant mustache was missing. The loose-limbed swagger had a purposeful side as he reached for the trailing leash.

"Matty, come. That's enough!"

*Who in the world is this?* Meg Ryan in person? A pixie in purple? Her gloves matched her eyes. Purple boots and everything packaged nicely in between. And she owns that monster?

"Miss, can't you control your dog?"

"Me? Matty looks to be running free, too. You ever hear of a leash law?" Even at five foot five, she had to crank her neck to glare toward his face.

Thane grabbed both leashes and handed her the blue one. "Your dog, Miss."

"His name is Harley and he and Matty have been walking buddies for months. Where is Josie, is she all right?" She barely kept from patting her chest in the hopes of slowing her heart.

Easy, man. This one is dynamite. Thane took a step back. "Why is everyone so interested in Josie? Can't a man walk his own dog?"

Blythe swallowed. His voice flowed like rich fudge syrup drizzling down the sides of vanilla ice cream. "You own Matty?"

"Why is that so surprising?" He reached down and patted her fawn head. The minx sat at his feet like she'd never had a dream, even of hightailing it across the marshes to sniff noses with her friend.

Blythe looked down at Harley who now gazed up at her, adoration in his eyes, innocence dripping from his lolling tongue, his tricolored body vibrating with the joy of being with her.

He always did guilt well.

"I'm Thane Davidson." Please don't tell me you're married.

"Blythe Stensrude." She stuck out her gloved hand. "I'm pleased to meet you. Any friend of Matty's is a friend of mine." Oh brother, how inane. Come on mind, let's work. Surely she wasn't standing on a charging battery or anything. She almost glanced down to make sure packed dirt held her up.

"So you usually walk with Matty and Josie?"

"Often, when I can get away." She gathered Harley's leash into one hand and stroked his head. "This is Harley."

"Harley the tank?" He eyed the broad shoulders and deep chest. "When he barked I thought it must be a mastiff or something."

"Or something is right. He usually doesn't get away like that." She felt his gaze travel down to her muddy knee.

"He dragged you?"

"No, more like flew me like a kite." She stroked her dog's rust colored head. Rust dots on white decorated his nose. Anything to keep her shaking hand busy.

"He's a handsome dog."

"Thank you. I've always thought Matty was a beauty." *Come now, there must be more to talk about than our dogs.* "Pardon me, but I need to keep walking so I can get back to work." She started up the path toward the duck pond.

"What do you do?" He fell in beside her.

"I'm a graphic artist." *Now, why don't I have any business cards with me? The first rule of networking—always have business cards in your pocket.* She checked out her pockets. *A disintegrating tissue, big help. Besides, she was a graphic designer. Why had she said artist?*

He strolled beside her, both dogs now dutifully walking slightly ahead of their owners so they could point out good sniffing places to each other.

"And you?"

"Troubleshooter for software companies."

*Surely not a computer geek. He didn't fit the image at all.* The warmth from his side heated through her jacket and the long-sleeved, turtleneck sweater she wore underneath.

He shortened his steps. "You live near here?"

She nodded toward the houses climbing the western

hill above the road that followed the curve of the bay. "What about you?"

"A condo off Alhambra. I'm not home a lot so that makes it easier. You interested in a latte? There's a place by the old train station." Now that popped out before thinking. Thane Davidson, what is the matter with you?

*Oh yes, oh no, I can't, I have to finish that project. If I say no, will I ever see him again?*

Say yes. Perhaps coffee will kick my mind into some kind of rational ability to carry on a conversation. After all, it's a simple latte? *Isn't it?*

# CHAPTER FOUR

"Sugar-free vanilla syrup, please."

Thane smiled down at his companion. "Not straight up, eh?"

"Nope, but extra espresso. I need all the help I can get." Blythe waved two fingers at the perky blonde behind the counter.

"Make mine a double, no syrup."

"Latte?" The smile she gave him had ramped up the voltage.

"Yes."

She wrote the instructions on the cups and disappeared behind the espresso machine.

"So why the extra caffeine?"

"I've got deadlines up to here," Blythe said, waving her hand over her head. And tonight will most likely be sleepless. But that wasn't something she really wanted to share with this striking hunk of manhood. Better to come across as capable. She'd been accused of flakiness in the past, more than once if she were to be honest. Amazing how slights of years ago still pained like barbs under the skin. She'd heard enough dumb blonde jokes to write a book of them and every one of them managed to irk her. Not that she was always a blonde, but it was the principle of the thing. As if the color of one's hair had anything to do with brain power. Or common sense for that matter.

Both of which she knew she had in plenteous supply, except when it came to succumbing to the pleadings of her regular clients, in spite of the sign on her wall that read, "You running behind does not constitute an emergency for me."

While these thoughts skipped through her mind like deer over fences, she kept her lashes covering the interest she knew showed in her eyes. Who would have thought a runaway dog could have brought such a man into her life? She reached down to pat Harley's head as he sat right by her knee, the perfect picture of doggy obedience. Thank you, hound dog, thank you.

They took their lattes outside and strolled between single-story brick buildings to Main Street, turning right as if they'd done this many times before.

"So, tell me about your business." Thane smiled down at her.

She forced her attention from a smile that reminded her of twinkling Christmas lights. Come on brain, a simple answer would be sufficient, promptly would help.

"How long have you been a graphic artist?"

"Ah, forever." She shook her head. "No, as my own business for five years now. I'm really more a designer than artist. I mean I do projects for other people, not like creating my own art. Mostly advertising." Why don't you stutter and stammer like a real airhead?

"And you love what you do?"

She nodded. "Usually, but right now everyone needs their things finished by Christmas. You know how that is. Time gets away." After another sip, she asked, "How about you? What is it you do?"

"My company goes in to fix mainframe computer problems for midsized companies. Interfacing programs, not so much hardware but software."

"Do you write software, too?"

"I can but that's not usually the case. More like puzzle solving."

"Did you like puzzles as a kid?" She glanced up at him. When he smiled, his right cheek creased in a dimple.

"Was there anything else?"

"Computer games?"

"Death to the invaders." He waved his latte like a sword.

"You still play them?"

"No, not really. I'd rather solve real puzzles." He took a swig of cooling coffee. "What do you do when you're not up to your hairline in deadlines?"

"I love music, my church…"

"What kind and where do you go?"

"Everything but heavy metal and acid rock. Oh, I don't care much for rap, either—hate the violence. I attend the Alhambra Community Church, have all my life. One of the things I need to finish are the programs for the singing Christmas tree. Do you like music?"

"About the same as you, but heavy on the classical side."

"Really? Are you going to the sing-along Messiah concert?"

"Hadn't thought about it."

"Are you a sports fan?" Every guy loved to talk about sports.

"When I have time. You?"

"My family is divided."

"Divided?"

"Mom and I love the A's, Dad and my sister are bone-deep Giants fans. Good thing they rarely play each other during the regular season or there might be bloodshed at our house."

"Surely you jest."

"I might be stretching it a little, but you get the point."

"Did you get tickets to the Bay Bridge World Series games?"

"No, World Series tickets are out of our league." She tipped her head in a sort of shrug. "And after the earthquake, we were glad we stayed home."

"Clients give me tickets to a game now and then. Maybe we could go sometime."

"I'd never turn down a ball game. You like football better?"

"Not really. I just don't have a lot of time to keep up with any team."

"So, you're a workaholic?"

"That's a rather offensive word."

"Sorry." Hey, it takes one to see one and on the plus

side, workaholics rarely want kids. Her inner voice tried to join the conversation.

"I do what needs to be done." His eyebrows drew together, eyes narrowing.

Touchy subject. What might be safer? "Look at those two, trotting along like they've never broken free, just well-mannered dogs out for some air."

"Bassets, ya gotta love them."

"How old is Matty?"

"Three. I thought about showing her, but even with a trainer…"

"It took up too much time?"

Blythe glanced ahead. End of walk coming up soon. "Read any good books lately?" She'd have missed his shrug if she hadn't glanced in the passing window.

"I don't read a lot for pleasure."

Why am I not surprised? She stopped at the corner of Alhambra. "We go up the hill." Draining her cup, she tossed it in the trash. "Thanks for the latte and the visit."

"I'm taking Matty home and going to Briones for a run. Are you interested?"

"I wish I could, not that I'm much good on the hills." She chewed on her lower lip. "No, I better not." *Please ask me for something else. I've got an extra ticket to the concert, will you go?* Her mother's voice blasted her. *Nice girls do not ask men on a date.* This nice girl hasn't gone on a real date, as in asked out by the man, for who knows how long.

"See you in the morning then?"

"The morning?"

"Walking the dogs." He smiled that lazy, megawatt smile again.

"Ah, sure." The sun came back out. "Eightish?"

"Good." He waved and started south.

"Come on, Harley, we've got work to do." She waved and headed across the street. Would she ever see him again?

"Blythe."

She caught her toe on the curb and half stumbled. "Yes?"

"I'll call you. You're in the book, right?"

"Yes." The sun brightened indeed.

"Good—see you."

She waved again and tugged on the leash. "Come on, dog, we got lots to do."

Harley dragged his feet, looking over his shoulder as his friend trotted up the street.

"Sorry, dog, but you'll see Matty tomorrow." That is— if her owner lives up to his word and if I'm able to sleep-walk down there.

Harley only stopped her twice for smell breaks as they climbed the hill toward home, her mind on the man, not the dog.

While she hung up her coat and Harley's leash, she thought of calling her sister to share the good news. I've met a man, a triple-scoop kind of guy and you didn't even have to find him for me. But then, what if he didn't call? How embarrassing. No, how normal. That thought brought her back to earth with a teeth jarring jolt. That same thing had happened far too often. But this time there had been chemistry. The tingle kind and surely not just on her part.

She sighed and plunked herself down in front of the computer. Get to work and quit daydreaming. If he calls, great. If he shows, greater. If not. Chalk up another one in the loser column.

Several hours and as many cups of tea later, she twisted in her chair, trying to pull out the kinks. She headed for another potty stop, then on to the kitchen to check out the fridge. She dragged a hand through hair that wore the dragged hands look and whooshed out a breath. Harley stopped at the back door, glanced over his shoulder and when she didn't respond, gave a gentle woof reminder.

"Just a minute." She pulled a bag of grated cheese and another of flour tortillas from the interior and set them on the counter. The dog woofed again, sharper this time. "I'm coming, you know patience is a virtue." His wagging tail bruised her shins as she passed him to open the door. "I should get you a doggy door but half the wildlife of the area could come in without invitation if I did." Ears flapping, he charged down the steps and across the back lawn to the doggy area she'd covered in wood chips. Her backyard really needed some help, as in tearing out the summer annuals and weeds that littered the curved beds. A rose camellia dropped rain-rusted petals on the bark underneath the shrub, the boxwood next to it wearing dying camellia blossoms among the small evergreen leaves. Perhaps she should hire someone to come in and do fall cleanup before spring came.

"Come on, Harley, I have work to do."

Bassets lose their hearing when their nose snuffles ground smells. She knew that to be so. But hope springs eternal and all that. "Harley! If I have to come get you…" He'd always ignored her dire threats and today was no different. "Fine." She shut the door and returned to fix her lunch, spreading cheese on the tortilla, putting it on a paper towel and into the microwave.

A sharp bark announced the dog's change of mind.

"Now you have to wait."

The phone rang. Could it be him? Mr. Sam Elliott look-alike himself? She crossed her fingers, all the while scolding herself for being so childish. "Blythe's Graphics. How can I help you?" She made sure her smile was in place. "Hi, Mom. No, sorry I haven't checked my machine. Forgot to." She cradled the phone between ear and shoulder and pulled her quesadilla from the oven, all the while mentally castigating herself for not checking the machine. She always checked the machine immediately upon returning home. After all, some important client might have called.

But when she checked the display of her answering machine, one call, and that would have been her mother's, was all there was. She listened to her mother, juggled the hot food onto a plate, and poured herself tea over ice. "I know, but there is no chance I can come this weekend. Mom, I'm sorry." She ignored her mother's remonstrances. "I know it's my birthday tomorrow…I'm going to skip it this year. Listen to me, please. I have work to do, as in some very important, very tight deadlines including the programs for the singing Christmas tree, so I am gluing myself to my chair. Make me a list and I'll see how I can fit it in. No, I cannot go out to the Christmas tree farm with the entire family." I'm not putting up a tree, I'm either canceling or postponing Christmas this year. But she didn't dare tell her mother that—yet.

"I'm sorry." She rolled her eyes skyward. What part of *no* didn't her mother understand? Understand? Ha, she didn't even hear it. "Look, I've had my break and I have to get back to work. Call you soon. Bye." Blythe hung up the phone on her mother's stutter and, plate in one hand, glass in the other, paused at the door, juggled, let the dog in and headed for her office. Harley danced at her side, his happy grin telling her he was sure going to enjoy sharing the treat she'd made. She set the food on the desk and herself in the chair, tapping the space bar to call up her work again.

Nothing. She moved the mouse. Nothing. The screen had frozen. "Not today!" Her shriek made Harley drop to the floor, eyes pleading as only basset eyes can, tail barely brushing the carpet.

"Okay, Blythe, take a deep breath, that's right, let it out, shoulders relaxed." That was about as helpful as moving the mouse. She followed her instructions once more and felt a bit of air between her shoulders and her ears. Again. If only her heart would settle down like her shoulders were doing.

She swallowed, ordered herself again to relax and hit control, alt, delete. Right, her program was not responding; now wasn't that a surprise? Control, alt, delete again and nothing happened. Not today, please not today. I should have defragged it. *Okay, Lord please fix this thing and not later, but right now. I need to work today.* She glared over at the old computer on a table across the room that looked as if Hurricane Ivan had passed through it. Being a horizontal sorter instead of a vertical one inclined to take up a lot of space. At least she had a backup machine. But when had she last backed up the files in question?

Her screen went dark. Not good. It hadn't followed the normal procedure for shutting down. *Lord, I thought you said you would answer when I called. Well, I've been calling and all I see is a dead computer.* Her stomach twisted itself in a half hitch.

Her hand automatically reached for the ringing phone, but she stopped before answering it. Right now was not a good time to talk to a client, or her mother or a friend, or anyone. The machine could pick it up. What was wrong with the computer?

"Hi, this is Thane Davidson." He had the kind of voice that sounded good even on an answering machine.

He called—like he said he would. A man who lived up to his word. And a computer genius.

She picked up the phone. "Hang on, the message will click off in a minute." She glanced down to meet Harley's expectant gaze, gave him a bit of her lunch and smiled when the machine clicked off. "Hi." Brilliant conversationalist that she was. "How was your run?"

"Good. How's the work going?"

"Not good right now. My computer is acting up." She pressed the start button, having given the monster time to sort itself out. But when it groaned instead of booting up, she felt like pounding it with something solid. Like a baseball bat. Calling it names failed to help, either.

"What's happening?"

"Can you hear it?" She held the receiver close to the tower.

"Yes. Pathetic." For the next half hour he talked her through various labyrinths of her computer, places she'd never seen nor had any desire to see again. Finally, he sighed. "How old is your computer?"

"Not quite two years."

"How long since you did a backup disk?"

"Two days ago. I do a complete backup every Saturday. And the file I was working on, I have the backup from last night. But the four hours I spent on it today will probably be gone, right?"

"Afraid so, sorry. Do you have program disks to reinstall?"

"Somewhere."

"What will you do? New computer or put in another hard drive?"

"Any suggestions?"

"Well, if you'd like, we could install a new hard drive, increase your memory and speed, not difficult."

"You said we."

"How about I get the hardware and bring it over? While you make dinner, I can get it up and running again. That is if that's what you want to do?"

While he was talking her mind flitted through her cupboards, freezer and refrigerator. What could she make? Or she could go pick up a barbequed chicken at the market, bake potatoes in the microwave and make a salad. A loaf of sourdough bread from the bakery would be perfect.

"Good. And thanks in advance."

"You are most welcome. Give me some information on your computer and I'll be on my way."

Blythe hung up, torn between delight at seeing him again and so soon, and despair at what she'd lost. If only they could retrieve that file. If only she had saved to the CD when she stopped for lunch. If only the hours went by more slowly. And here she'd been thrilled to be as far along as she was. Was being the operative word. She glanced around the office. No time to clean that up but then a clean office was the sign of a sick mind, another sign on the wall said so and she totally believed it. Until someone else was coming into her office.

She moved the backup disks of the files she'd been working on over to the other computer and booted it up. While he worked on one, she could be working on the other. It was just slower than a weary snail.

Harley moved, too, laying down with his chin on her foot, his normal place during the working day, if there were no sunspots to bake in. Blythe leaned down to pet him.

"Sorry, buddy but there won't be any playing today." She leaned her head toward one shoulder, let it stretch, and then to the other, trying to pull the tension from her shoulders.

*Why, oh, why didn't I save that file? I know better.* She glared at the dead box on her other table. Should have taken a baseball bat to it just for the pure joy of it. And how was she to fix a company dinner on top of this?

"Come on, Harley, we're going to the store." If the man thought he might get home cooking, he would be in for a surprise. *I wish I knew if he is in a relationship. You never can be too sure these days.*

# CHAPTER FIVE

Thane caught himself whistling as he opened the car door for Matty.

How long since he'd whistled? Something that used to be part of his daily life. When had it gone away? How surprising that he'd noticed. Something was in the air, that was for sure.

He slammed the rear door of his SUV and opened the driver's side. "I think, dear Matty, that I have found the woman of my dreams." He glanced over his shoulder to see his hound sitting on the seat just behind the passenger seat. "I thought I put you in the back." Her ears went down and her tail stopped. "Oh, all right. Sit there. But don't you bark when I go in the store." Her tan polka-dotted front feet danced on the leather seat and she gave him an adoring look, before shifting to watch out the window.

Purchasing the needed computer supplies took less time than he'd thought it would, so when he followed the instructions of his GPS, and knocked at Blythe's door, no one answered. If she was so hot to finish her work, where had she gone? Obviously she'd not taken Harley—his deep woof from the other side of the locked door announced that. Thane turned and stared around the neighborhood, a mishmash of cottages, some redone, others deteriorating but in a genteel manner. What had once been a working class neighborhood now showed traces of yuppie invasion.

"If you're Thane, she went to the store," a woman two doors down called.

And if I'm not Thane, did she not go to the store? Were there other neighbors spying as well? No one was peeking out of windows, nor skulking around corners of the houses. "Thanks." He returned to his vehicle and debated; take Matty for a walk, go back home and work for awhile, or stay here and check for messages. The latter won out and with Matty giving his other ear a quick cleaning, he dialed for messages and set about answering what he could. Change of schedule for tomorrow. He glared at his cell phone. Now he wouldn't be able to walk Matty in the morning or invite Blythe out to dinner. Half tempted to say he wasn't free in the morning, he dialed back and agreed. One did not renege on one's largest client, even though he'd need to be on the road by 5:00 a.m. to beat the traffic and get to South San Francisco by eight.

He left a message on Josie's pager that he would need her to walk the dog in the morning and late afternoon. At the next message he shrugged, checked his PalmPilot and set the meeting for Thursday at noon, definitely time to walk and latte before leaving—and for that trip, he'd take

BART so he could work on the way home, as long as he got a seat. The Bay Area Rapid Transit sometimes seemed like a second office, and the sights of all the other computers and technical devices showed that others used their travel time as wisely as he did. He'd never learned to sleep on the commuter train.

He was just finishing his last message when a well-cared-for older car turned into the drive just behind him. Perfect timing. He scooped up his purchases, popped the rear door and went around to grab Matty's leash as she jumped to the ground. While he had to boost her over the tailgate getting in, she leaped out with a happy woof.

"Hope you don't mind my bringing her?"

"Not at all." Blythe reached into the back seat for several plastic bags. "I didn't expect you so soon."

Harley's woof turned into a full-blown howl.

"Your friend is not a happy house sitter." He followed her to the yellow front door. Pots of geraniums lined the three steps to a porch shadowed pink through the western screen of bougainvillea. A white wicker rocker with a cushion splashed in vivid reds, pinks and yellows had already invited him to sit and make himself comfortable before he opted to work in the car.

Not that wicker was his thing. His outdoor furniture lacked cushions over the teak slats, mainly because cushions needed to be taken in and he'd not taken time for such mundane things.

He waited while Blythe fumbled with the key, finally opening the door to a rush of Harley, yipping his greeting to Matty, entirely ignoring the man looming behind his owner.

"Some watchdog, isn't he?" Blythe motioned Thane inside. "Welcome. Let me put these things in the kitchen and then I'll show you the way to my office."

"Okay, dogs. That's enough sniffing." He raised his voice slightly to follow Blythe. "Do you mind if I take Matty off the leash. She has good house manners."

"No, of course not."

He glanced around the room as he unsnapped the leash and folded it to put in the pocket of his leather bomber jacket. Lived-in but lovely and inviting. Just what he'd expect of the woman who so intrigued him. She might call herself a graphic designer but she could add interior decorator and artist to her list as the two oil paintings—one of the waterfront at the park, the other of John Muir House out toward the freeway—both bore her signature. A trio of watercolors of summer blooming irises, purple cone flower and Mexican sage showed her artistic versatility. If she'd also taken the photos lined on the mantel, what was she doing producing playbills, menus and advertising for local businesses?

"There, sorry I took so long." Blythe wiped her hands on her jeans as she entered the room.

"You did all these?" He nodded to all the artwork.

"Ah, yeah." She shrugged as if they were of no account, as if anyone could create such beauty.

"I see." Keep out of her business, Davidson, you have enough of your own. He picked up the packages. "Let's see your computer."

She led him down a stair lined with what he assumed were family photos interspersed with more art shots and lots of Harley. Harley sleeping, Harley running toward her through a field of California poppies, Harley looking up from nose digging, his muzzle covered in dirt, Harley as a puppy wearing reindeer ears at Christmas and a woebegone expression.

Matty and Harley both followed behind them.

Blythe pointed to the newer computer on a desk against the far wall. On one wall, sliding glass doors led the way out to the backyard and two computers sat on a table off to the right. A drafting table took up space in the middle of a room with one corner set up with easel and paints, and another with framing supplies of a mat cutter, clamps and a miter box. Tools hung on the wall above it.

"You're a jack of all trades?"

"Yeah, and master of none."

"Doesn't look that way to me."

"I'll turn on the computer. Now that someone is here who understands it better than I, it will probably work just fine."

"Please." He shook his head, raising very expressive eyebrows to go along with the slightly sarcastic word.

"Don't you know that mechanical and technical things always behave for one in the know? Like cars for a mechanic?"

Thane rolled his eyes and removed a tool kit from his jacket pocket before removing said jacket and hanging it on the back of a chair. How like a woman to anthropomorphize even a computer. "They are nothing but a box, chips and circuits."

"Frequently run by gremlins who delight in messing around with said circuits and chips. Not a lot they can do with the box. But keyboards and a mouse, that's another gremlin family, I'm sure."

He shrugged and pushed the power button. Nothing. "Guess it really is down."

"Not that I like to say I told you so, but…"

"Have you ever taken a computer apart?"

"Once, when I added more memory."

He pulled out the tower and began to unplug cables, whistling a tune under his breath.

"Would you mind if I go work on the other one?"

"Uh, of course not. Just stay close so I can ask you questions if I need to."

"Dinner will be ready anytime we are."

He nodded and removed the first of the screws. As usual when confronted with a failed computer, he lost all track of time and space, rebuilding the insides, and putting it back together. "These the installation disks?"

"Those to your right, yes."

"Okay."

After a bit, he asked her more questions about how she wanted programs installed, and when she came to stand behind him, the light fragrance of her perfume reminded him of summer days and citrus drinks.

"I can do the rest."

"If I do this, can you get further ahead on the other?"

"Well, yes."

"Good, then let me help." He looked over his shoulder. "If you don't mind."

"Mind?" She shook her head. "Why would I mind? I just hate to take advantage of you." Her cheeks flushed pink when she realized what she'd said.

He kept his chuckle inside.

"I mean." It was her turn to roll her eyes. "Oh good grief…" Her cheeks deepened in hue. "I think I better go check on our dinner." She fled up the stairs, both dogs jumping up to follow her.

Thane watched her go, chuckled and turned back to the computer. After all, he had to earn his dinner. The old saw, sing for his supper, drifted through his mind. Now *that* would take away anyone's appetite. Shower singing was his forte. Matty often howled along with him.

While he heard Blythe come back down the stairs, he kept his focus on the work he was doing. About half an hour later, he nodded and whooshed out a breath. "You want to come check this?"

"Really? You're done?"

"Hope so." He stood and motioned her to the chair. "Try it and see." He stood behind her after she sat and watched her nimble fingers dance over the keys, bringing up screen after screen.

"It is faster, that's for sure." Her smile made him want to lay his hands on her shoulders. "Looks like I just have to redo what I've done and while I'm not back to where I was yet, I soon will be."

Turquoise eyes—I never believed there was such a thing. He smiled back at her. "Then I suggest we eat and Matty and I will get out of here and let you get back to work."

"Yes, of course." She broke eye contact and pushed back her chair—slowly so as not to bump into him. "I'll never be able to thank you enough."

"Sure you can, by letting me take you out to dinner on Saturday."

She spun her chair around. "Wait a minute, that's not me paying you back. I should take you out to dinner."

"I asked first."

"Thane Davidson, you have a weird sense of humor."

"Good, then humor me."

Banter through dinner is good for one's digestion. Thane glanced at the woman across the table. When had he enjoyed a simple meal more? The thought of the good time they were sharing, besides being good for his digestion, his stomach informed him of that, melted the steel out of his shoulders and business concerns from his mind. Matty shoving her nose under his arm made him glance at the clock.

No wonder—her mealtime had long passed.

Thane laid his napkin on the table. "My friend here just reminded me what time it is. I need to be going so you can go back to work. Unless of course you are done for the evening."

"No, I'm not. My client needs that project tomorrow. I had planned on having it done tonight."

"No grace period?"

"'Fraid not."

Thane stood. "Thanks for such a good evening."

"Thank you for the computer repair."

Thane felt his phone vibrating in his pocket. He

checked the lit screen. "I need to get this, so I'll be on my way. Come on, Matty. Say goodbye."

He snagged his jacket and tool kit from the wingback chair where he'd left them and headed for the door. "See you."

He glanced back to see Blythe waving from the back-lit doorway, Harley at her side.

"As I told you before, Matty, m'dear, that is one special woman. You think there's any special man in her life? She'd not indicated as such. I wonder what kind of flowers she likes best."

Matty whined and looked out the window.

# CHAPTER SIX

I still don't know if he is in some kind of relationship.

Blythe closed the door and turned to feed her four-footed, for-sure friend. There never was any doubt of their relationship, just occasional questions as to who was really in charge.

So why didn't you ask? The voice on her shoulder must have just awakened from an extended nap.

"Because I'm chicken, that's why. Although why would he go out of his way to help me if he had a girlfriend? Wouldn't she be jealous?" She set Harley's dried dog kibbles, topped with a spoonful of canned food, on the rug by his water dish. "Okay, have at it." Teaching him to wait for permission to eat had taken a lot of training, one of the few things she'd followed through on. "Good dog." I'd be jealous. If I heard about it, that is. So many men are so sneaky these days. As in Henderson, who'd married her good friend. Somehow the friendship had died at the same time.

Blythe couldn't stomach either lying or cheating, never had been able to, even when the excuses were believable.

"So the next time I will ask him."

The next time what? *That voice again.*

"The next time we are together." Which would hopefully be in the morning in the park. One did not ask life-altering questions over the phone where one could not watch the eyes and entire body language. She sighed and headed back down the stairs to her office—and a computer that now worked. Had she said thank-you enough?

Blythe turned off the computer at 3:03 a.m. and was in bed and asleep by 3:05 a.m., or close to it. *Thank you, Father,* was her last thought. The project was finished. When the alarm rang at seven, she smashed the snooze button twice before staggering to the kitchen for her first cup of coffee. At least she had thought to prep the coffeemaker the night before on one of her breaks. Coffee mug in hand, the fumes helping to alert the part of her mind that screamed for more sleep, she sipped her way to the bathroom for a shower. If only she could take her caffeine by IV in the morning.

She donned her robe, stepped from the shower and stared into the mirror. Today is my birthday. I am now officially thirty years old—and still single. Eyes as tired as hers did not belong on a thirty-year-old, more like someone sixty, or forty anyway. She blinked, smiled, patted her cheeks. "Come on, girl, get yourself in gear."

Harley licked drops of water off her leg, then walked to the door and whined. He looked over his shoulder as if asking what was taking her so long. There were sniffs to be sniffed and rabbit or gopher holes to investigate. He wagged his tail and yipped.

"I'm coming." She moussed her hair, finger-combed it into her typical disarray and smoothed moisturizer over her face. "I had better get more faithful on a beauty regimen if I don't want the wrinkles to take up permanent residence." Harley flopped down with a sigh. "Harley, I sure wish you understood the importance of birthdays."

Toast in one hand and leash in the other, they started for the marina within a half hour. She'd not missed eight by much. But no other basset escorted an owner around the paths or out on the pier. He said he'd be here. Perhaps he overslept, too. Or he had to take a call. Or—this thought was the killer. He'd shined her on. "No."

Harley raised his head.

"Not you, boy. Just talking to myself, which I seem to be doing more and more lately." She picked up their pace. "Come on, dog, let's get this over with. I have an in-box full of work." All the while they jogged the park's paths, she kept watching for Thane and Matty. By the time she and Harley reached home, both of them fought to catch their breath and she couldn't pant without her tongue hanging out. What a way to spend the first part of her birthday morning. After all, he had said he'd see her in the morning. "And I didn't even get a latte."

Most women by age thirty had little children to make mom's day special. The thought struck terror and fear to her heart. Do not go there, she ordered her capricious mind.

Only her mother called to wish her happy birthday.

"Thanks, Mom. No, I'm not doing anything special, I just don't have time. Next year."

"But this is your thirtieth."

"Don't remind me, I'm trying to forget. Oh, and speaking of forgetting, I'm not doing Christmas this year." She held the phone away from her ear until her mother calmed down. "Of course I'll come to your house for Christmas Day, I'm not that hard-hearted. And I already have most of the presents." She didn't tell her mother she'd had them wrapped at the stores, again to save a chunk of time.

"Please, Mom, I feel bad enough already. Lighten up, will you?" After a few more comments and a couple of pregnant silences, they hung up. "Well, that went a long way toward making me feel better."

Some birthday. No cake and not even an ice-cream bar in the freezer. No kiddies to help blow out candles. What is the matter with me today? Two cards in the mail. Of course, she'd said she was going to skip it, but still... Not even her sister remembered her supposedly special day. On one hand she was grateful for the quiet phone and on the other...sigh. Brad had picked up his project at ten and now that it was nearly dusk, she stood at the window, watching fog sneak up the river. The day had flown by. Tail in the air, nose skimming the ground, Harley quartered the backyard, checking to make certain what animals had invaded his territory. He followed one trail to the fence. Most likely the neighbor's cat had used the flower bed under the window for a litter box.

After a quick dinner of ramen soup, she headed back to her lair where the stack had dwindled but the remaining projects were not the garden variety, one-day type. Her birthday had gone virtually unnoticed, the one man who'd promised to meet her for a latte didn't and she had a headache. Some day. Good thing each day was still only twenty-four hours long.

I thought Thane might be a possibility. Only he never showed up, never called. *Father God, I thought You were on my side*. Perhaps it was best this way, especially if he was a man who might want children. She'd never put herself in a situation like that again.

She let Harley out for a last run, turned out the lights in her office and headed for the claw-footed bathtub in her bathroom. One thing she would do was treat herself to a long, healing soak with bubble bath, aromatic candles and soothing music.

But when she turned the CD player on, the strains of "Silent Night" filled the steamy room. Ignoring the tears streaming down her face, she tested the hot water. Overworked, overwhelmed, underappreciated and no Christmas.

# CHAPTER SEVEN

"Where is she?"

Thane stopped, Matty at his heels. She sat and looked up at him, adoration evident in every quiver of her sturdy body. From the top of the bridge over the Alhambra Creek, he scanned the entire waterfront. Plenty of people, strollers, joggers, bikers, dog walkers, but not one purple-coated pixie with a tricolored basset.

So, did you come just to see her or to walk your dog, giving you both some needed exercise? Interior monologues could be so disgusting, so brutally honest.

He struck off across the marsh at a good clip until Matty whined and pulled back on the leash. "Sorry, girl." He waited while she did her business, not needing the plastic bag he kept in his pocket for cleanup, and headed back toward home. He didn't bother to stop for a latte—somehow without her there to enjoy it with him, the coffeepot at home sounded just fine, or at least adequate. Halfway home, he dialed her number on his cell.

"Blythe's Graphics. Sorry I cannot…" Argh. How he hated answering machines. But when she didn't break in, he dutifully left his message, including both cell and home phone numbers and ending with, "I'll see you about 6:30 then. I'm hoping you like sushi, I made reservations in Walnut Creek but we can cancel and go somewhere else if you want."

After a shower and still no response, he thumbed through the yellow pages for the number of the local florist, the one on Main Street that they'd walked by the other day. What kind of flowers would she enjoy the most?

He placed an order for a mixed bouquet to be delivered asap and booted up his computer. She wasn't the only one with work to do.

"All that work and he's still not happy with it." Blythe slammed the heel of her hand against the steering wheel. How she'd kept her cool in the meeting with her client was still a mystery to her. "I'll know it when I see it. It's just not there yet." Famous last words. And here she thought she'd done just what he described.

At least her birthday was over and she could go on getting older without feeling like she was voted least favorite and forgotten, friend or relative.

Sure, why don't you throw a pity party all for yourself. You're the one who said you were too busy, remember? There was that dreaded voice on her shoulder. Why did it always have to be right?

*Sorry, God, I'm not being very grateful, am I? On one hand I pray for work, then You send it my way and I grum-*

*ble. Surely there must be some kind of balance, some-*
*where.*

I wonder if Thane was down at the marina? The
thought made her wait too long after the traffic light
turned green and she got a honk to wake her up.

"Sorry." She fluttered her hand by way of apology
and drove on.

Harley greeted her at the door, spinning in circles, ears
flying. She bent down to pet him, telling him what a good
dog he was and how lonesome the house would be without him. She'd just hung up her jacket and was heading
for the back door to let Harley out when the front door bell
chimed.

"Just a minute, dog…" But he beat her to the door, his
bark announcing unknown company.

Blythe checked through the peephole to see a person
hiding behind flowers. Pulling open the door, she gasped,
"How beautiful."

"If you're Blythe Stensrude, these are for you."

"I am." Flowers, who would send me flowers? Probably my sister since she forgot my birthday. She took the
flowers, inhaling lily, carnation and mum flavors. "Thank
you so much." Shutting the door with one foot, she carried the arrangement to the coffee-table and pushed aside
the two coffee-table books to set the flowers in the middle. Or maybe they would do better on the dining room
table. Or would she see them better in the kitchen? Down
in my office would be best. But for the present, she'd leave
them where they were. Brightening up her living room.

Harley woofed at the back door.

"Sorry, dog. I'm coming." She pulled the card off the plastic holder and went to let the dog out.

"Thane Davidson! Oh my…" Stars and garters is what her grandmother used to say, or the even more general purpose phrase used by many Norwegians, *uff da*. Yes, this surely was an *uff da* moment.

She sank into the overstuffed chair and propped her elbows on her knees, the better to inhale and study her flowers at the same time. Her fingers itched to get out the watercolors. To capture the burgundy and white mums, the needles and cones of the evergreen branches and the glory of the fire-throated lilies.

She read the card for the third time.

"To remind you that I'll see you soon. Ever, Thane Davidson."

"Guess we're on for dinner all right." She turned to see the message light blinking. Harley yipped to come in. She inhaled one more burst of beauty and went to let in the dog. First things first.

Dog in, she retrieved her camera from the closet and quickly snapped pictures from every angle. She would get to paint them, even if not right now.

That done, she pushed the button on the answering machine.

"Blythe, this is Thane Davidson…" As if she wouldn't have recognized his voice. "Ready by… Oh my word, girl, you better get in high gear. And yes, you sweetheart of a man, I love sushi."

She whirled once around the living room, Harley staring at her as if she'd lost her mind.

Amazing how one's mind could kick into high gear when the timeline shortened–nothing like anticipation to fire one up.

Four hours of work, one to get ready. Ah, there was the catch. What to wear? How to get her hair to stand and lay just right, how to touch up a broken nail, put three outfits back in the closet after they failed the "to wear or not to wear" test. Once she decided on the pink pants with the swirly pink, turquoise and purple shirt, she couldn't find the right earrings. "How can I lose my favorite earrings?"

Harley melted further into the rug, only eyes and brows moving in response to her flitting about.

"I know you hate for me to be gone but it won't be for long. I'm just going out to dinner. Actually, I'm being taken out to dinner by a real man who lives up to his word." She sang the last words. "Well, most of the time anyway. Or at least one out of two." And she possibly would have seen him this morning if she'd gone on down to the marina like Harley wanted. But after today, she could deliver the programs to the church in the morning—getting them printed was someone else's job.

She belted the big shirt, added bracelets, changed her mind on both belt and bracelets, dug out others and breathed a sigh of relief when the doorbell rang. Now she couldn't change her mind again.

"The man in black." She invited him in with a sweep of her hand. Wearing a black turtleneck, cashmere, for sure, black slacks and a black leather bomber jacket, the man shouldn't be allowed out in society. He'd devastate the female population.

"Is something wrong?" One eyebrow arched higher.

"No, w-why?" She caught the stammer. Please mouth, work right.

"You look a bit shocky."

"Oh, sorry." Shocky right, you took my breath away. She glanced up—and up—to look into dark eyes that crinkled at the edges, eyes easy to drown in. "I, ah…" She couldn't talk, her words snagged by her dry throat and held prisoner. Without volition, she leaned closer.

"You are so incredible." His whisper shivered down her spine and up again.

Kissable, his carved lips were surely kissable. *Blythe Marie Stensrude, you do not kiss on the first date, so back off.* She ignored the woof at her feet but when Harley let loose with a full basset howl, they both stepped back, looked down at the howling dog and burst into laughter.

"Now that's the best chaperone I ever saw." Thane leaned over to stroke Harley's head. "Sorry fellah, if I intruded on your territory, but it's all right, my intentions are honorable."

Blythe retrieved her coat from the closet. "Puppy treat, Harley?" She felt like she should pat her chest to quiet her still racing heart. She took her overly warm face into the kitchen, Harley prancing beside her. Scooping two small biscuits out of the box, she leaned over and kissed the top of his head. "Thanks, dog. You saved me from myself." Harley munched the treats while she dug a new braided circle chew treat from the stash and handed him that. "Now you stay out of trouble."

As she entered the living room where Thane waited, her gaze fell on the flowers. "Oh, Thane, forgive me. I forgot to thank you for the flowers. They are glorious."

"You are welcome and no forgiveness necessary. I'm glad you like them."

"Like them? I love them." She slid her arms into the sleeves of the coat he was holding. The warmth of his hands when he rested them for a moment on her shoulders invited her to lean back into his chest, but she reached for her purse instead. This man could be addictive, that was for sure.

She locked the door behind them and turned, biting her lip. "I have to ask you something really important but I don't want to offend you, either."

"All right." He waited on the walk, three steps down, light from the streetlamp picking up a few strands of silver in his dark hair.

"Ah." Just get it over with, dummy. Her words came out in a rush. "Are you married or ever have been?"

"No and no. And you?"

She bit back a retort. "No and no. Nor engaged, either." Nor even a serious relationship. "Just dated."

"What fools men are if they just dated you."

"I think we better go." Her voice squeaked on a gulp. In the driveway Blythe eyed the step up into the deep blue Land Rover. Good thing I didn't wear a straight skirt.

"I can make it kneel if you want."

"That's all right." She reached for the handle between windshield and door and pulled herself up and onto the seat. Somewhat different from her little car all right.

"Here's your seat belt." Warmth leaped the distance between their fingers as she accepted his thoughtfulness.

Fanning herself would look way out of character, so she clicked the end of the belt into the receiver and sat, face forward.

Never in her life had a man affected her like this. She and her friends had joked about chemistry, but this was no laughing matter.

"So, how are your deadlines coming?" He shoulder checked both ways before backing out.

"Making good progress—mostly."

"Mostly?"

She told him about her difficult client, which led to a swapping of horror stories about demanding clients and had them both laughing on the drive to the restaurant.

"Thanks again for fixing my computer. My regular repairman only just got back into town today. I would have been hung out to dry."

"Glad I was there." He parked the SUV in the back of the parking lot. "Have you eaten here before?"

"No, but I've heard good things about it."

When he realized she had to trot to keep pace, he slowed and tucked her arm in his. "Sorry." She had no answer, but her smile said it all.

She wanted to stop and inspect the marvelous wood carving of a dragon that sat in the center of the room, but followed their waitress to the black lacquered table she indicated.

"Do you have any favorites?" Thane laid the open menu on the table.

"I don't know the Japanese names, but I love the prawn one, the California roll when it's like an ice-cream cone, and crispy salmon skin. So you choose." His fluid use of the Japanese names and the smiles he exchanged with the waitress impressed them both.

"You've been to Japan?"

"A few times." He motioned to the teapot just set on the table. "Tea?"

"Yes, please."

He poured, then separated his chopsticks and rubbed them against each other to remove any slivers.

A silence caught them by surprise. Let's see, he's not interested in sports. "You have family around here?"

He shook his head, a frown flitting across his face. "No, my parents were killed in a plane crash."

"Oh, I'm so sorry. Do you have any siblings?"

"One." His jaw clenched and his eyes narrowed.

Whoops, better not go there. Get your foot out of your mouth, Blythe, and take a sip of your tea. That's safe.

"How did you happen to get a basset?" Thane asked.

Safe subject. "We had one as kids. You know the Fred Basset cartoon?"

Thane nodded. "Fits the breed pretty well, I'd say."

"Well, we had a real Fred. Two years ago, I read about a basset at the local rescue shelter then went and adopted him. The man who'd owned him had a fixation with Harley motorcycles, thus the name."

"He's a handsome dog."

"Thanks. Did you have bassets before?"

"Nope. I saw Matty…" He glanced up as the dish of

soybeans was set before them. "Thank you." He pushed it closer to her. "Help yourself."

"Thanks." Blythe took one of the pods and scraped it between her teeth, chewing the soy beans thoughtfully. "So was Matty a puppy?"

"Half grown. My sister had to move and couldn't keep a dog in the next place."

She watched his eyes in the dim light and flickering candle. There was something more behind this that he wasn't telling.

"She sure turned into a beauty."

When the server set their trays of sushi on the table, they mixed the green wasabi with soy sauce and dug in, Thane identifying those pieces she didn't recognize.

By the time they left the restaurant, Blythe knew more about sushi than she thought she would ever need to, but questions about his family burned to be asked.

*Please, ask me out again. You could invite him to church in the morning. But he…* The mental argument picked up where it had left off earlier.

"What are you doing tomorrow?"

"Working, after church that is. I have to take the Christmas programs in."

"You finished those."

"Sure did. Perhaps you'd like to come with me."

He paused, as if giving her invitation serious thought. "I better not, perhaps another time."

Better than nothing.

"I saw a birthday card on your mantel. When was

your birthday?" He slowed down and turned into her short driveway.

"Friday."

"And you spent it working all day?"

"That's the breaks."

He shook his head. "We'll have to do something special to celebrate, even if it is late." He stepped from the car and came around to help her out, then guided her up the walk with a hand just touching her back.

Do I ask him to come in? No, too late. Harley barked from inside.

"Your watchdog." He looked down at her, then leaned forward and lightly brushed his lips across hers. "I never believed in love at first sight."

"Me, either."

"Good night." He stepped back.

She dug her keys out of her purse and floated up the steps. "Night. And thank you for a marvelous evening."

"You're welcome." He touched a finger to his forehead and returned to the truck.

So did his comment mean he now believes in love at first sight or…?

"I'm coming, Harley, hang on to your collar."

# CHAPTER EIGHT

I wish he were going to church with me.

Harley yipped at the back door.

"I'm coming." She threw the bedcovers back with a sigh. Staying in her daydreams would have been nicer, but dogs didn't understand that. She touched her mouth and could still feel the gentle brush of Thane's lips. And his parting comment, "I used to not believe in love at first sight." No, that wasn't exactly the way he said it, but was the upshot that now he did believe in love at first sight?

Intellectually she knew true love grew over a long period of time, but attraction could double whammy one instant quick. Lord, let him be a believer. I think he is but what do I know? She set the coffee maker to work, let the dog back in and wandered to stand at the front window where sun cast stripes and shadows on the carpet through half-opened slats. It didn't pack the zest of a summer sun, to be sure, but a blustery winter day was indeed invigorating. And besides, she might see him this afternoon.

The coffee machine beeped. She fixed Harley's breakfast, much to his tail-wagging delight, poured herself a cup of coffee and danced and twirled to her bedroom to dress for church. Much as she preferred the ten o'clock service, today she would do the 8:30. *Ah, Lord, I have so much to be thankful for. If this could be the man you meant for me, please make it clear. I don't want to make a mistake. But, oh, how special he makes me feel.*

Sitting in church some time later, she wished again he were sitting beside her. Would they go to this church or his? Does he have a church? Another major question to ask. So much to learn.

Keeping her mind on the music was not hard, for she loved to sing. Keeping her mind on the sermon, now that was a different matter. Finally she forced herself to take notes on the border of the bulletin. *To love the Lord my God with all my heart, soul, strength and mind. Ah, how I want that. To love my neighbor as myself. Loving my neighbor wouldn't be hard in Thane's case.* She caught a giggle before it reached her mouth.

With a sigh of relief she stood for the closing hymn. Now to deliver her folder of camera-ready copy for the singing Christmas tree program. Since this was an event offered to the community, they always needed hundreds of programs. The church would be standing room only for all three performances.

She slid through the crowd, exchanging greetings but not stopping to chat. If she could get four hours of work in, she wouldn't feel so guilty being gone for an hour or two.

A blinking light on the answering machine greeted her return home. Please let it be Thane. She crossed her fingers as she played the messages, after greeting an ecstatic Harley. You'd think she'd been gone for days instead of two hours.

"Sorry, Blythe, I'm going to have to cancel for today. I've got an emergency in the city. I'll call you later if I can get out of there early enough to do dinner, that is, if you'd like to. I had a great time last night, thank you."

Blythe sank onto a chair with a sigh. Rats and double rats. Harley put his paws up on her knees and peered into her face. His droopy eyes made her smile and rub his ears. "Not your fault, Harley, boy. So much for a fun afternoon. Now I'm just going to have to work all day. Which is probably best, but still." She kissed the top of his head and pushed against his chest. "You get down now, so I can get going."

The afternoon slid by with only two phone calls and neither of them from Thane. Her sister Suzanne, apologized for missing her birthday. Blythe mentioned she had met a man, kind of slid the comment in under the general conversation.

Her sister finished her story, paused, started to say something, then paused again. "What was that you said? Did you mention the word 'man'?"

"Yes." Blythe rolled her lips together to keep from giggling.

"And you are seeing this man?"

"Yes." And is he ever easy on the eyes.

"Blythe Marie Stensrude, quit the games and tell all."

Her voice took on a big sister commanding tone. "Where did you meet him and what is his name?"

"Well, actually, Harley met him first." She didn't mentioned the loose dog fiasco.

"Blythe, if I have to come over there and drag the story out of you, I will." Suzanne waited. "I know, let's do a girls' night out and…"

"I can't."

"Blythe, honey, this is Sunday, a day of rest. You are not supposed to be working on Sunday."

Guilt made Blythe hunch her shoulders. "I know, but I have too much to do. But that isn't why I can't join you."

"It better be good."

"How come when I suggest a girls' night out, you always have a million excuses and I'm supposed to just understand?" Her sister's favorite phrase: "you understand, I know."

"Sorry, but this is different."

"You'll have to understand this time. Thane said he'd figure something for dinner if he could get away in time."

"You mean you're just sitting there waiting for this guy to call?"

"Hardly. I need to get back to my friend, the computer."

"No way. His full name?"

"Thane Davidson, I met him at the marina. He was walking his basset named Matty. Harley and I walk with Josie, the dog walker I told you about. She walks Matty. I just hadn't met Matty's owner before." But I have now and I'd rather go out with him than you, sorry, dear sister.

"Harley likes him?"

"Yes, he does."

"Okay, sweetie, but you better keep me posted. Have you told Mom yet?"

"Nope and don't you, either. This man is not ready to pass the Mom quiz. Or the family gathering. So don't nag at me."

"*Moi?* Nag?"

"Bye, Suz." Blythe hung up and headed for the kitchen to make a cup of tea. Red Zinger sounded good about now.

But Thane didn't call that afternoon or that evening.

"So, he couldn't get away. We know how that is, huh, dog?"

Harley whapped her calf with his tail as he spun around, before heading for the back door.

"All right." She let him out for a last run and fixed herself another cup of herbal tea. Any caffeine now and she could kiss sleep goodbye, no matter how tired she was. She pulled open the freezer and studied the ice-cream choices—she'd stocked up since her birthday. Six ice-cream pint cartons lined up two deep. Vanilla with chocolate almonds, vanilla bean, jamocha almond fudge, strawberry and chocolate chocolate chip. How to choose? She tested each carton to see which was lightest. Vanilla bean won out so she pulled a jar of fudge sauce from the fridge and set it in the microwave to warm. Nothing like a hot fudge sundae on a Sunday evening. She fixed Harley a small bowl without the fudge. Now if only that phone call would come.

They settled in the living room for a movie on the Hallmark channel. Harley finished his ice cream and nosed the dish around, licking it until the dishwasher couldn't have washed it better. She ate hers slowly, savoring every bite. Maybe she should call him just to chat. Maybe not. He didn't seem the chat-on-the-phone kind of guy. When the movie came on and she saw men riding across the hills with guns to the ready, she switched it off. Even if it had been Sam Elliott.

She met with clients in the morning, leaving some finished projects and picking up new ones, dropped books off at the library, picked up cleaning at the cleaners and went by the bank to make a deposit. Back at the office, she returned phone calls, accepting one job and turning the next one down.

"Sorry, I just can't meet that tight a deadline." Mentally she patted herself on the back. Wish I could talk with Thane about it. How had that thought leaped in? Funny how thoughts of him had a way of sneaking in when she least expected it. Not that she ever really expected it. This was new to her. *Father, keep him safe and help him work out whatever is taking up his time.*

"Come on, Harley, we need a walk." All along the paths she hoped to see him or hear Matty, but that was silly. He only came down in the morning. Tuesday morning they walked at eight. No man and no dog. You could call him, you know. Sure and if he acts like he's never met me, then what. She buried herself in work to close off that argument, but a snobby voice whispered, you're just a fraidy-cat.

By Wednesday, she'd slammed the door on every

thought of him, including prayers. He'd started out great. So had some of the others.

"Uh-oh." June locked her fists on her hips as Blythe and Harley strode by. "Things took a nosedive."

"I got tired of blond." On the hour she'd allowed herself for lunch, she went to the store, picked out a box of hair color, and did the deed.

"Uh-huh, and you be courtin' the wee folk with yer new Irish look."

*Sorry, your accent isn't right yet.* But just because she was feeling snippy, no need to take it out on someone else. "Do you like it?" She doffed her smash hat and fluffed her hair with her fingers. Today was warm enough that she didn't need gloves, or a hat really, either.

"Must be the sun that's makin' it look like a halo of fire."

"A wash or two and it'll lighten up. You want to walk with us?"

"Thankee, but me own work be callin' me."

"When's your first performance?"

Harley tugged on the leash, leaning as far forward as he could with his front feet planted.

"Right after New Year's. I'll get you tickets."

"Thanks." *You think they'll let Harley in?*

They made a fast trip through the park, again empty of Thane and Matty, ignored the latte stand and punished the pavement home. More and more she stretched the old adage, hard work cures a broken heart. Not that she was going to allow a man to break her heart. Not now. Not ever.

She returned the call from her mother that had been on the machine.

"We have your Christmas tree, dear, when should Dad bring it over?"

"Mother, I told you, I'm not doing Christmas this year. I'll just enjoy the tree at your house on Christmas Day." And if there was any way of getting out of that, I'd do it.

# CHAPTER NINE

*So you're here today. So, do I care?*

Harley tugged on the leash, back feet scrabbling on the gravel.

*Sure dog, you see your best friend and you want to go running to her. You don't care that you haven't seen her for five days and she didn't even call.*

*Maybe I ought to learn something from my dog.*

Being dragged along by a basset in full strength was not a pretty picture, she was sure. Planting her feet did no good and since she didn't want to go airborne, she donned a mantel of dignity and strolled—well, not exactly strolled. Harley had her nearly jogging, but giving the impression of strolling seemed to be important at the moment.

Matty was obviously doing the same thing. Thane didn't seem to be resisting like she was.

"Good morning." His greeting sounded like he'd seen her the day before.

How was she to get cheer back in her voice? Was she glad to see him? Not necessarily. She'd just talked herself out of looking for him, wanting to see him, hear his voice…to yell at him for letting her down just like all the others had. Oh, to be able to ignore the leap of her heart. Be still had about as much effect as telling Harley to stop, sit or quit barking.

She plastered a smile on her face and glanced down at the dogs who were sniffing, yipping and bouncing, their joy bubbling and bursting.

"Blythe, what? Ah, you look different."

She looked up to see straps of a backpack digging into his shoulders. What is going on? He brought his breakfast along? "Sorry. Good morning to you, too." Although there's not much good in it yet.

"You dyed your hair."

"Yeah, well, I do that sometimes."

He turned so she could see the child in the backpack, a little girl by the pink stocking hat. Had he been holding out on her? The child stared at her, one finger in her mouth, her cheek against Thane's back.

"I'd like you to meet my niece, Amie. She's three and not too happy at the moment."

She looked like she'd been crying, eyes red, mouth drooping. "I see. Hi, Amie."

The little girl sniffed and turned her face the other way.

Blythe felt like doing the same, but curiosity had a head-lock on her now. Where is her mother? He said niece, so this was not his daughter. Relief lightened the weights on her cheeks and eyes. Questions rose like steam from a kettle.

"Shall we walk?"

Blythe nodded and fell in step beside him, going back
the way she'd come. But before they could take three
steps, she bent down to untangle the dog leashes. Taking
a moment to gather her fragmented mind, she patted both
dogs and sweet-talked them, receiving quick licks and de-
lighted wiggles in return.

When she straightened back up, she caught him watching her. A smile that started with the right corner of his
mouth, slowly spread to include his whole mouth and finally reached his eyes made her catch her breath. What was
it shining in his eyes? Sure seemed like the look her father
saved especially for her mother. Wasn't there an old song
about the "look of love"?

She swallowed and took in a shoulder-raising breath.
That look had zinged straight to her heart and set it to ket-
tle drumming. *I've missed you. Why didn't you call?*
"The dogs are sure happy." *Now.*

"One of these days I'll explain what all has happened."

She glanced up to see his jaw set again. There must be
some awful kind of trouble for him to have his niece. And
he must have had her overnight since they were together
this early in the morning. Her mind took off on all kinds
of possibilities.

"I'm taking some time off work until things settle
down. You have any experience with little girls?"

"Actually I have two nieces myself." She knew her
tone was guarded but discussions about children had never
been her forte. She glanced up at the child in the backpack. She had fallen asleep, thumb and finger still in her
mouth, eyelashes feathered on rounded cheeks.

"Amie is sound asleep."

"I shouldn't have thrown her into her clothes so fast but I wanted to meet you here."

"Has she had breakfast?"

"A cereal bar. I need to go shopping. Will you come?"

"I've never had children." *And I'm not taking a life-threatening chance like that.*

"I know—neither have I—but I thought perhaps together, we could, I mean, oh…" He paused and shook his head. "This poor little kid has been jerked around, her mom is gone and here she's stuck with me. I haven't seen her for six months and that's a long time in a life this short."

Amie woke with a jerk, whimpering, "Mommy? I want my Mommy." Tears threatened again.

"See what I mean?"

Blythe heard the misery in the child's voice and saw it on Thane's face. A fast rundown of her list of to-do's for the day made her groan inside. How could she find time to help out and yet make her deadlines? While her nieces adored her and she them, she hadn't gotten close until they were older. Small children—huh-uh.

"My house is not set up for this, I have as much of her things as I could fit in my SUV, the bed went on top. We made quite a picture driving up from San Diego."

"Unca Fane, I gotta go potty." She wriggled and sighed.

"Can you wait a…oh, no."

"What's wrong?" Blythe stepped back. "Oh." She could see a wet spot spreading on his back. The urge to giggle swept over her. She clapped a hand over her mouth to trap the rising laughter.

"I see no humor in this. I think we'll go home now." He picked up the pace, heading for the parked truck.

"Did you drive?" She turned and walked with him.

"Yes, the truck is in the parking lot by the pier."

"Well, I guess we'll see you later then."

"I'm serious. I really need some help, you know any good day care places?'

"You mean now?"

"You wouldn't ask if you saw my house."

Blythe thought of her morning's plan and gave up with a sigh. "I can manage a couple of hours. Why don't you drop me at my house, I'll put Harley in and follow you?"

"Blythe, I cannot begin to tell you how grateful I am." The look on his face confirmed his statement.

Amie whimpered as he swung his backpack off his shoulders. "Mommy coming?"

"No, baby, Mommy isn't coming. We'll get you home and…"

"I want Mommy."

The plea tore at Blythe's heart. *Did the mother die or—or what?*

"Did you bring any other clothes?"

"Not here." He flipped up the bar on the kiddie seat. "Here you go."

"I wet." She wrinkled her nose and shook her head.

"I'll fix that when we get home. Get in the car seat, please."

Matty leaped up on the seat. Amie shrieked and stumbled backwards, her cries echoing in the vehicle. "No, no, doggy bad. No!"

Do I take the dog or the child? Fearing to make the child worse, Blythe took hold of Matty's leash. "Come, Matty, there's a good girl."

"She's afraid of dogs, too. Right now, she's afraid of everything." Thane glanced over his shoulder to make sure Blythe heard him as he held the little girl close. "Easy, Amie, it's all right. Blythe has Matty and all you need to do is get in your chair so we can go home and clean you up."

Still sniffing, she finally did as asked, rubbing her eyes. "Mommy."

The whimper burrowed into Blythe's soul. Danger! Danger! This little one wanted her mommy and it wasn't her. She planned never to sign on to mommyhood. How long would Thane have the child and *what happened* to her mother? And while off to a rocky start, this relationship *had* been a possibility…a now dimming possibility.

Thane put Matty up in the back, behind a screen. "Now you stay, hear me?" Matty thumped her tail.

Telling Harley to stay is like telling Christmas not to come. Blythe reached down and stroked his head.

"Here, can you two share the front seat?"

"Of course." She motioned Harley to jump up to the floor, which he did just fine. Except he then scrambled up on the seat before she could climb in. He grinned at her, tail thwacking the console. "Down, Harley." She pointed to the floor. He looked down and then away, as if to say, you can't mean for me to sit down there. "I do mean it." She tugged on his leash. "Moving him is like shifting a concrete block."

"Get him out and I'll hold him until you get in, then he'll have to stay on the floor."

Blythe nodded. They could have been halfway home by now. She tugged on the leash. Harley planted his feet. "Harley, come." He wagged his tail and doggy-grinned.

Thane stepped around Blythe, scooped up the dog and set him on the ground. "Hand me the leash."

Blythe did so, climbed up in the SUV, leaning her knees toward the middle so Harley had room on the floor. Once inside, he looked at her like she'd betrayed him. *Good thing it's a short trip home. He's not going to like being left, either, but what can I do?*

Once he was home and engrossed in destroying a new chew bone, she returned to the truck, to hear Amie crying again. Matty whimpered from the back but before they made it to Alhambra, the dog broke into a howl. Amie looked over her shoulder, her cries cut off like someone threw a switch.

"Matty, that's enough."

Blythe watched Thane's jawline turn white.

The dog howl wound down to a whimper. The child sniffed and muttered, "Bad doggy."

"This scene would win funniest home videos."

"Thank you very much. I'm glad you don't own a camera."

"We could go back so I could get it, but you could never stage it to work again."

"You're not funny."

"Come on, Thane. This is one of those 'if you don't laugh, you're going to have to cry' times. It'll get better."

"Wait until you see my house."

He was right. Blythe stood in the doorway of what must have been a well-decorated bachelor pad, once. Black leather furniture and glass tables—strictly modern and utilitarian. Not a trace of family or color. Other than the painting over the fireplace. What might be three tulips against a background of layered oil paints that looked sculpted with a trowel, hung in solitary splendor. If one liked that kind of art.

Stuffed bears, dolls and a giraffe spilled out of boxes, a pink Big Wheel-style trike, jammies, pink overalls, shirts and a robe trailed from other boxes, hair bows and barrettes littered the smoked glass coffee table, a pink fleece blanket on the leather recliner, a juice glass on the counter.

"I put her bed up in my office. Now I have to move all the office equipment into my bedroom. We need a chest of drawers, all this put away and the closet is full of my business suits. I have nothing in the cupboards for a little girl to eat, and not much for me since I rarely eat at home. You begin to get a small piece of this puzzle?"

Amie ran for her blankie and, tucking it under her chin, climbed up on the sleek sofa.

Thane picked her up. "Let's get you dry before you sit there."

The wet spot made the leather look even darker.

Blythe headed for the kitchen, wet a paper towel and wiped down the leather. Surely the little girl hadn't sat there long enough to make the leather smell. What did one clean leather with? She found the trash in the pantry, tossed the towel and stared around. Where to start?

Thane walked back into the room, Amie walking beside him, hanging on to one of his fingers. Her blankie trailed behind.

"Perhaps we should go shopping. First a chest of drawers and a toy box, then a house." He shrugged at her shocked look. "Perhaps tomorrow for the house."

What kind of man is this? Blythe ignored his smile, hard as that was, and surveyed the mess. "We could stack these boxes against a wall for now."

"They were stacked, until I needed to find clothes for her and she insisted on a bear to sleep with. The blanket wasn't sufficient." He leaned over to pat his dog. "Oh, and did I tell you? I hate clutter."

"Far as I know, clutter comes with kids, part of the package. Let's move this stuff to the other room, the bike could go out on your deck. We'll go buy the furniture and then begin the shuffle."

"Who'll watch Amie while we shop?"

"We take her with us."

The look of shock made him appear more like other earthly men.

Amie dug in one box and pulled out a well-loved doll, missing one arm. She started toward the sofa. Matty trotted over and grabbed a corner of the blanket hanging off the sofa. Tail wagging, she headed for her bed in the corner, the pink square dragging behind.

Amie let out a shriek, threw the doll down and ran for her blankie. Matty charged under the dining table, hanging on to her prize, tail up, declaring this a wonderful new game.

"Drop it, Matty." Thane's order might as well have been smoke.

Amie dove under the table, Matty charged down the hall, blankie in full flight.

"You get the kid, I'll get the dog."

"Not on your life. You get the child, I'll get the dog." Blythe charged down the hall after Matty, into a bedroom the size of her living room with a bed big enough for four. No dog. "Matty, where are you?" The walk-in closet was the size of most bathrooms, with everything hanging or folded neatly in its place, but had no dog. *He has more clothes than Imelda Marcos has shoes.* She backed out and shut the door. No dog in the royal bathroom, either. "Matty, where are you?"

Blythe got down on her knees and peered under the bed. Matty wagged her tail. "Come on, girl. Let the little one have her blankie." She could hear screaming coming from the living room. *Thank you, God, that I only have to worry about the dog.* She reached for the corner of the blanket nearest her and Matty growled. Not a warning growl, but a "let's play some more" growl.

Blythe collapsed on her stomach, giggling into her arms.

The screams died to whimpers and the whimpers sounded close. Blythe turned to look. Thane and child stood in the doorway.

"She won't come out."

"Matty, bones."

The dog charged out from under the bed, her tail whipping Blythe across the face.

"You just have to know the right words."

She spit dog hair out of her mouth, half crawled under the bed to reach the blanket and crawled back out. No one needs a bed that big anyway.

Back in the living room she handed Amie the blankie and received a glare in return as if she'd been the one hiding the treasure all the time. So much for good deeds.

Within an hour and a half they were back at the condo, where Thane called the manager to ask for help getting the new furniture up into his home. Besides the chest of drawers and a toy box, they had a bookshelf and a play table with two small chairs, all painted white.

While the men moved the office furniture, Blythe made peanut butter and jelly sandwiches for herself and Amie, then emptied the boxes into their proper places. She set the toddler to putting together a puzzle on the table, making sure that Matty didn't get into the act again, and put the living room and kitchen back to rights.

"Thanks, John." Thane waved the moving helper out the door and took a deep breath. "Thank you, it looks like I have my home back again. Are you a genius or what?"

Blythe finished a last swipe of the kitchen counter. "You're welcome. Now I need to get home and get to work."

"And leave me alone with—with them?"

"Them?"

"Matty, Amie, you know."

"Sorry, but I've got work to do. You said you were taking time off."

"I am. I've got to find some kind of day care. You wouldn't…"

"Nope, but you can call my sister. She knows about things like that." Blythe rattled off the phone number. How come a man who can run a company of his own and save all these companies' computer systems panics with something as simple as this? And yet, he'd never looked more endearing. Blythe blew him a kiss as she left.

# CHAPTER TEN

*Call her now, she needs a break.*

Thane almost hated to destroy the hard-earned peace and quiet by speaking aloud. Amie had finally fallen asleep, Matty's snores at his feet didn't count as noise, only one more piece of the peace and quiet. He stared at the Gary Larson calendar on his desk, a gift from his sister. She'd always tried to get him to lighten up, take time to smell the marigolds. He never had liked the fragrance of marigolds.

*Call her.* When his inside voice became so insistent, he usually heeded it. Red hair. Why had she dyed her hair red? What was wrong with blond? But then, what was her natural color? And did it matter?

He shook his head and punched the keys. Ten-thirty, surely she wasn't asleep yet. Not with all the work she'd had to do, and she'd taken out several valuable hours to help him. He well understood deadlines and fighting to keep one's head above water when building a company of your own.

"Come on, answer, don't let it go to the answering machine." Screening her calls, was she? Surely no clients called her at this time of night. "Pick up."

"Blythe's Graphics, I am away from the phone right now…" He listened to her message, fingers drumming a tattoo on his leather desk pad.

"Hey, Blythe, sorry to not catch you, just wanted…"

"Don't hang up. I'll turn the machine off."

Even the sound of her voice made him smile. She sounded breathless.

"Sorry about that. I had my head in the oven."

"Blythe, surely you're not… I mean, is it a gas range?" I knew she was feeling overwhelmed, but surely she isn't depressed to that point.

Her chuckle warmed him clear to his toes. And relaxed his shoulders.

"It's electric and self-cleaning, but I was wiping out the ashes from running the clean cycle. Did you think I…?" Her laugh trilled.

"Just being cautious. And now that I've given you your laugh for the evening—I wanted to thank you for all your help today."

"You did look on the verge of panic. Be right back, Harley wants in."

He closed his eyes while he waited, the better to picture her. She wasn't the type he usually dated, as if there'd been any "usually" for more than the last year.

"Sorry for the interruption."

"Dogs don't wait. Nor do little girls." He sighed.

"Hard day?"

"You were here, but let me tell you, it is easier with two people."

"I can guess."

"I think I owe you an apology." He cleared his throat. "You know when we met in the park?"

"Yes."

"You were pretty frosty at first. I got to thinking later that perhaps you were upset that I disappeared for four days without calling."

"Five."

"Ah, yeah. Well, I got caught in a hurricane named LynnEllen. She's my sister and ever since Mom and Dad died, has been either drunk or high most of the time. Fortunately she'd been clean and sober for several months before she conceived Amie, so we don't have a fetal alcohol baby on top of the rest. She called last week to invite me down to San Diego for Christmas, said the last rehab was working and she wanted Amie to know that she does have a family." He leaned back and propped his feet up on the desk. "Then last Sunday night I got a call from her again. She'd been picked up, violated her parole and was back in the slammer. Could I come down and get Amie? LynnEllen swears the crack found in her car wasn't hers, but she's been a liar for so long, I can't believe her. She'll be in for life due to the three strikes law if she is convicted. So I hired a moving van to take her things to storage for now, packed up Amie and brought her here. You know the story from there."

"Oh, Thane, how awful."

"I was so angry at her, at the whole mess she's made

of her life, I couldn't lay that on anyone, least of all you. And as you can see, Amie takes up all the time I have. I get furious all over again every time she cries for her mommy. And on top of that, she and Matty are not hitting it off. She's afraid of dogs, she's afraid of the dark, she screams if I leave the room."

"It's called separation anxiety. Harley had a bad case of it when I first got him."

"Working on a computer with a child sitting on your knee just doesn't work." He sighed again. This seemed to be a night for sighing.

"Did you call my sister?"

"Not yet. I will in the morning. I made an appointment with a Realtor to go looking at houses."

"You were serious."

"Of course, there's no yard for her to play in here and if I decide to find a nanny, I'll need a bedroom for her, too." He glanced over to his inviting bed. "Having my office in my bedroom reminds me of my college days."

"Where did you go to school?"

"Stanford. Got my MBA at Berkeley. What about you?"

"California College of the Arts at the city campus."

"In San Francisco?"

"Yes. I loved it there. My wild and free days." Blythe drove her fingers through her hair, now gelled to stand upright.

"I can't picture you wild. Free, yes, because you are."

"You think I'm free?" Her laugh made him smile in return.

"Free enough to change your hair color. That was a bit of a shock."

"Not to those who know me well."

I want to be one of those. I want to know you better than anyone does. "I'm learning."

"Yeah, you are." The tone of her voice made him smile. He stroked his chin with one forefinger.

"I've been thinking."

"And?"

"And I need to make sure Amie has a good Christmas but I have nothing here to even start with. You think you could find time to help me?"

"But I'm not doing Christmas this year."

"Neither was I." He waited, giving her time to think about it. *Please agree to help me, please.*

"You're not going to move before Christmas are you?"

"No, even if I were to find something tomorrow, closing takes longer than a week." He eyed the calendar. "Unless…"

"If you want me to help, you have to promise no moving before Christmas."

"I promise." He raised his hand. "Scout's honor."

"Uh, Thane, I think there is something I should tell you…"

Amie screamed, the sound raising the hair on the back of his neck. "Gotta go. Amie. Bye."

Matty barked and howled from her crate, banging against the door, as upset as he was.

"I'm coming, baby. Hang on." Heart pounding, he entered the room lit by a Pooh Bear nightlight and picked up the screaming child. "Easy, sweetheart, easy." He held her to his shoulder and slowly paced the room. "What woke you up?"

She hiccuped, wrapping both arms around his neck. "Bad things."

"Nightmares?"

"Mommy coming?"

"No, but Uncle Thane is here." He strolled down the hall, patting her back and crooning in her sweaty ear. "Easy, Amie, all is well now."

Sometime later with both of his charges settled down again, he sank into his favorite chair and stared out the window to see the lights of Martinez and the black stretch that was the river. *Lord, I thought I was on the right track, with my company and my time. But You really threw in a clinker here. This is more than I can handle.* He rubbed his hands through his hair and nodded. Good point, eh? How long had it been since he'd opened his Bible? Attended church regularly. Prayed more than brief bursts for help, or of thanks.

"It's not like I have a lot of time." What a lame excuse. He blew out a sigh. Often when he felt like this, he'd go running, it didn't matter what time of day or night, he'd just go. But now, now he was stuck and it was all Linnie's fault.

Somehow he couldn't generate the rage he'd felt while in San Diego and driving home. While he might feel confined, she was in prison. "Linnie, how could you be so stupid? You knew better!" He thumped his hand on the arm of his chair. *Here I am with your child.*

"And you are all alone." He whispered the words.

"What they said they found—that's not my stash." She'd said the words so firmly, her eyes locked on his, no blinking, no turning away. "I have not gone back on my word, I've been clean and sober for three months now."

Talking on a phone through bulletproof glass, her voice had sounded tinny. But she never wavered. And yet, they had found a stash of crack in her car, under the front seat. How had that gotten there?

Around and around, thoughts in a maze, finding no answers, only more questions, he finally pushed himself upright and went to bed. At least Blythe would help him. Surely they could pull off Christmas in two weeks. Now if he could only find a good sitter. You didn't shop for presents with Amie along.

When the doorbell rang at 8:30 a.m., he was just taking Amie out of the tub. The laundry was piling up, Matty needed a potty run and he couldn't leave Amie alone so he had to bundle her up to go out. He wrapped her in a thick navy bathsheet and, with one end trailing, answered the door.

"Mr. Davidson?" The smiling man behind the noble fir looked vaguely familiar.

"Yes."

"Blythe, my daughter, said I should deliver the Christmas tree we cut for her here instead of her place. I'm Arne Stensrude."

"Ah, ah, good, come right on in. We can put it out on the balcony for now." He stepped back to make room, accidentally stepping on Matty's foot. She yipped, he jumped away. If this was the way the day was going to go, all he wanted to do was go back to bed. If he ever needed a triple-strength latte, it was now.

# CHAPTER ELEVEN

"Hey, little sister, how's the love life?"

Blythe sighed. Leave it to Suzanne. "Nothing like getting right to the point. What happened to 'hi, how you doing?' Or something like that." She wished she hadn't answered. Or that she had one of those machines that showed who the caller was. Or let her machine pick it up like she'd been doing for the last week.

"Your fault, you haven't returned my calls."

"Sorry. I got busy and forgot."

"So, you got your decorations up?"

No, I told you. I'm not doing Christmas. Remember?

"Dad said he took the tree over to Thane's. Did you know he called me about day care?"

"I gave him your number. I sure don't know anything about it." And don't plan to learn.

"Far as I know there's nothing available until after the New Year. Is he going to adopt Amie?"

"I don't know."

"I agreed that his idea of a nanny is the most possible, so he's putting an ad in the paper."

"Good."

"Something wrong?"

"Nothing that ten more hours a day wouldn't fix." Blythe eyed the stacks of projects on the table. Working bits of time here and there just wasn't effective. She needed long stretches so her brain could calm down and lock into the ideas. Thane had missed their walk again this morning. He said getting Amie ready that early was nearly impossible. Understanding and acceptance didn't have even a nodding acquaintance for her, nor for Harley, either. She was beginning to think the man was taking too much of her time, at least thoughts of him were. Maybe she should back away.

"Not to change the subject or anything, have you decided what to get Mom and Dad?"

"I'm thinking of tickets for a cruise. You want to go in with me?"

"That would be pretty spendy." Suzanne paused and Blythe knew she was figuring out the possibilities. "Sorry, sis, I don't see how I can do that much. What about a weekend in a B and B up in the Gold Country."

"That sounds good. You want to look into it or me?"

"You're better on the computer than I am."

Blythe knew her sister was up to her eyebrows with the kids' activities and church and the singing Christmas tree. She let out a sigh. "All right." *Sometime between midnight and dawn I'll do it.*

When they hung up, Blythe rested her head in her hands.

Harley put his front feet up on her thigh and nosed at her near hand. When she ignored him, he nosed harder and whined.

"Ouch, your toenails are digging in." She pushed him away but when he dropped to the floor and gave her his most sad and dejected look, she shook her head. Leaning down, she rubbed his ears and head, enjoying as always the silky feel of his soft hair. "You need a bath. You want to go to the groomers? I just do not have time to give you a bath."

Quickly, before anything else could interfere, she called Doggy Palace and booked a grooming for him on Monday. Unlike her, they weren't open on Sundays.

She checked her messages and clicked off the phone ringer in her office. The machine would have to do its job. Several hours later, deep in the design for a booklet for a local charity, she floated up to hear, "Blythe, pick up. I know you're there." The voice sounded impatient and very male. *Thane, didn't you get the point?* But his insistence on getting her attention made a smile come out to play.

She hit "voice" so she could have her hands free. "I'm working."

"I could tell. But you need a break."

"No, I don't need a break." Harley heard her talking and barked at the back door.

"Harley says you do. Thanks for the tree. It is a beauty."

"Mom and Dad always cut beautiful trees." *I don't have time to chitchat.* And yet she found herself leaning back in her chair and smiling for no reason. "Do you have a stand for it?"

"No. But I'll get one."

"Decorations?"

"Nope, but listen, I looked at several houses and there are three that I would like you to look at."

"Why? I'm not buying the house."

"Just because you have excellent design sense and know more about kids than I do."

"Thane, I've never had children, either." *And I don't plan to, the risk is too great. I'm not to be trusted alone with babies and small children.*

"Not plural. One is more than I can handle. But right now she is cuddled in my lap, looking at a book."

The picture of them flashed through her mind, bringing a clench to her middle. If Amie was sitting on his lap, she must be calming down. Blythe glanced over to her painting corner. What a study they would make. She jerked her concentration back to the conversation.

"You want me to what?"

"I said, how about if we go look at those houses in an hour or so since I have to make a bid on one or the other before they are sold."

"You can't decide on a house that fast. You have to look around and compare."

"Not in this market. It's buy or be gone. Then we could go buy some ornaments and decorate the tree. Amie can help us. Please?"

"Thane, it's not manly to wheedle."

"If it works…"

She laughed in spite of herself. "Oh, all right." After all, it is for Christmas and a little child. *So much for sticking to your guns, what a marshmallow you are.*

She finished the part she was working on, closed down the program and heard Harley barking. *Good thing it's nice out, I forgot all about him. If the neighbors are home I'm going to hear about it.* She let him in, poured his dry dog food in his dish, added the bit of canned and set it down. "I know it's early but I might be late and then you'd eat the house."

She dug the Christmas boxes out of the storage room next to her office and lugged them up to the car, making sure she had the tree stand that held plenty of water. A quick check in the mirror had her pull a purple cotton knit sweater over her tailored shirt. Her jeans were fine, she just added earrings and a gold chain, and touched up her makeup.

"You behave now, Harley. I'll be home later."

He stared at her, ears down, tail down, eyes pleading to go with her.

"Sorry, if that child screams at Matty, what will she do with two of you? Maybe next time." She found him a chew and threw it down the hall.

Once at Thane's building she hauled out the tree stand and took the elevator to his floor. The other doors all sported wreaths or decorations of some kind—perhaps they could pick up a fresh swag at Navlets, a local garden shop. She rang the doorbell, actually humming a carol she'd heard at the grocery store.

Amie seemed to have become an appendage on his right arm but at least she wasn't screaming. Matty yipped her pleasure at seeing Blythe, then looked around as if asking where her buddy was.

"Come in." Thane stepped back. "We've even picked up our toys for company."

Is that the royal we or has he already fallen into the parent trap? "So, does that mean you picked up the toys and she supervised?" Blythe smiled at the little girl. "Hi, Amie."

Amie turned her face into Thane's shoulder.

So much for remembering me. Figured. Blythe held out the stand. "I brought this up but there are more boxes in the car."

"Boxes?"

"Of decorations. I wasn't going to use them so I thought perhaps it would save a shopping trip."

"You are to be called a woman among the blessed." He shrugged. "Well, I messed that verse up, but you get the point." He set Amie down and checked out the stand. "I thought to put the tree in front of the doors to the balcony. Cooler there and I can block off that heat vent." He cocked an eyebrow, waiting for her response.

"Ah, great." Don't look at me like that. For some insane reason, she felt an urge to stroke his cheek. What would a real kiss feel like? The quick brush of his earlier one had created all kinds of sensations.

"Unca Dane, juice please?" Amie tugged at his pant leg.

"Sure, sweetheart, let me see how this is going to fit." He eyeballed the stand before stepping out on the balcony to do the same with the tree trunk.

"Unca Dane, now." A whine joined up with a quivering bottom lip.

This child knows how to work the system. Blythe bit back a smile. "I'll get you some juice."

"No. Unca Dane."

"Amie, let Blythe get your juice. There's a carton in the refrigerator."

The whine picked up force, like a tropical storm being upgraded to hurricane status. One tear slipped down her cheek, before that innocent little mouth opened up and a cry loud enough to wake the neighbors burst forth.

Matty headed for her crate. Thane set the tree very precisely back against the wall and closed the door behind him. The glint in his eye and the set of his head told Blythe for sure there was something to dread.

"Amie, you cannot have juice when you are crying." His voice slowed and deepened.

The little one cranked up the volume.

"Okay, kiddo, time out." He picked her up, crossed the room to the corner and sat her on a chair. "Now, stay there until I tell you to move."

She immediately flipped her little self over and slid off the chair, the look over her shoulder daring him to do it again.

*I can see this is going to be a fun evening. Talk about two strong-willed people.* Blythe opened the door. "I'll go get the boxes. Perhaps your manager has a dolly." Before he could say anything, she shut the door behind her.

By the time she'd hauled the three boxes up to the condo, Amie, red-eyed but subdued, sat sipping juice from a sippy cup. Thane had the tree in the stand and waited for her to hold it while he tightened the screws.

"I did it by myself but nearly knocked the thing over, so…"

Blythe eyeballed the tree straight and held it while he finished securing the tree.

She stepped back. "It is a lovely tree, even without decorations."

"It is." He turned to Amie. "Get your coat and hat."

"Go get Mommy?"

He shook his head. "I have the backpack in the car. Marlo is meeting us, I'll call her from the cell."

Amie dragged out her pink fleece blankie.

"I said your jacket and hat."

"Gone."

"You can't find it?"

"Uh-huh."

Thane marched to her room and returned with jacket and hat, plus her bear. He held it for her to put her arms in, then zipped the front. Hat on, she looked like a pixie out for a dance. He bussed her cheek when he picked her up, making her giggle, the first giggle Blythe had heard from the little girl. As she'd figured, Unca Dane was indeed a wonder. At least with those of the feminine persuasion.

They drove out Alhambra Valley Road where the big homes were. Thane introduced her to Marlo, a woman Blythe recognized from the Chamber of Commerce meetings she seldom attended any longer. All the places had five bedrooms and acreage, along with vaulted ceilings, the latest in gadgets and hefty price tags. One was brand-new, the others a couple of years old and their landscaping finished.

"So, what do you think?" Thane asked when they completed the last tour.

"They're all beautiful. The one with the attic above the garage would be good for a nanny's apartment." Blythe thought a moment. "Do you want unlived in or…?"

"Doesn't matter, although I'm not much for yard work. The one with the room above the garage also had the best pool design and the pool house could make a nice office." He jiggled Amie in the backpack.

Blythe walked over and looked out the window of the house they were in, giving him a chance to talk with the Realtor. Such space both inside and out. Fenced yard for both dog and girl. Not that she could see the need for so much house, but then he is probably planning for a family someday. Although he has a family already, even though they weren't daddy and daughter.

Did she know any women to introduce him to? What about Marlo, she sure was turning on the charm? And she wasn't wearing a wedding band. For some strange reason that thought made her want to leave—now.

"Okay, I'll call you either later this evening or tomorrow morning."

"Fine. I'll look forward to hearing from you. Just don't wait too long and be prepared for a bidding war."

Yeah, you hope so. But Blythe smiled politely and let Thane help her up into the Land Rover after settling Amie in her car seat.

"So, which do you like the best?"

"Thane, that's not important, which do you like the best?"

"I love the view from the one higher up, but the land around that first one is more useable."

"Useable for what?"

"Oh, a barn if Amie wants a pony some day. Another garage if I take up a hobby."

"What kind of hobby would you like?"

"I don't know, haven't had time to think about it. But many people take up hobbies, I run now, but I know I don't want to play golf. There's room there for a volleyball court."

"You play volleyball?"

"Just for fun. I used to, in college."

The things she was learning.

They discussed the three houses, narrowed it down to two and bought a pizza to take back to his house. Blythe looked back to see Amie sound asleep in her car seat, bear tucked in her arm.

Thane carried her up and laid her on her bed, all without waking her. "She's one tired little girl. Here I thought she would help us decorate the tree." He removed her jacket and shoes and pulled the covers over her.

"No nightie?"

"Nope. Not tonight. Come on, let's eat."

Blythe paused by the bed to smile down at the soundly sleeping child. Amazing how such a determined little girl could look so peaceful in her sleep. But remember, motherhood is not for you, your careless act those years ago proved that, so lock away those maternal instincts that are trying to sneak out and go eat pizza.

Together they checked out the strings of lights, replaced a couple of the tiny white bulbs and, starting at the top, at Blythe's insistence, wrapped the tree from the inside out in twinkle lights.

"We have to do every branch?" His tone tended just the slightest to an adult male whine.

"Now you sound like Amie." Blythe wrapped the lights around the branches of the third layer from the top. "You want it to look nice, don't you?"

"I think I remember why I don't like putting up Christmas trees. I suppose you hang every piece of tinsel one strand at a time, too."

"I don't do tinsel. Hides the ornaments." She reached across the branch to hand him the lights and at his touch nearly dropped the loops of lights. They could well have been hot for all she could think. He looked as shocked as she felt. Warmth flowed from the top of her head to her toes. "Ah, do you—" she huffed out a sigh. "Ah, I mean you could wrap that branch if you would."

"Sure." His gaze never left her face.

They finished the lights and stood back as he flipped the switch on the cord. "No crawling under the tree to turn on the lights, never again."

Matty sniffed the tree branches, picked up a broken twig and laid down to chew on it.

"No, Matty, sorry, that's not for you." Her gaze followed him as he took it to the kitchen and dumped it in the trash.

Blythe brought her attention back to the tree, which kept her from following his progress, as his dog was doing. The seven foot noble fir could have been a ten-foot one in this room, but even so, the symmetry was perfect. She opened the boxes of ornaments and hung the first one on an upper branch.

"My grandmother made these for me." She held one of the ribbon-and-beaded creations up for him to see. "We'll be careful and put the prettiest and most fragile above where little fingers and doggy noses can't reach. My sister taught me that."

"How does Harley manage with the tree?"

"His tail can be lethal, so I do the same at home. The first year he ate a couple of ornaments so I make sure no glass ones are near the bottom. You'll see that there are felt and painted wooden ones I put down there." She hung another of her treasures and looked up to find him staring at her. "What?"

"Thank you for bringing all these. I probably would have gone down to a store, seen a tree that looked okay and told the clerk, 'I want all of those boxed and shipped.' Or even the entire tree if I thought a fake one would work."

"You wouldn't."

"One year when I had a company party at my house, I hired a florist to do the entire thing."

Blythe shook her head. "Christmas has always been my favorite season. I started early so I could enjoy every minute of it."

"So this year has been doubly hard."

"Yes." She sniffed. Surely she hadn't missed it enough to cry over it.

Thane set the star on top and they stepped back to admire their handiwork.

"I have cider in the fridge, can you stay long enough for a cup? Of course, heated in the microwave is not like homemade but…"

She smiled up at him. "It's the thought that counts."

"Sit down and I'll get it."

"I'll clean this up."

"No, I'll do that later. You sit." He pointed to the corner of the sofa.

"All right." She sank into the leather with a sigh. I better not sit too long or I'll fall asleep. Matty came over and laid her chin on Blythe's knee. "You are such a sweet dog." Rubbing the dog's ears and watching the tree made her feel like she was floating in peace.

"Here you go." He handed her a mug of cider, redolent with spices and a cinnamon stick to stir with.

"Thank you." She breathed in the fragrance. "I haven't done any baking or anything." So many beloved traditions gone by the way side. All because she took on too much work.

Thane set his mug on the table and sat down beside her, not quite touching but close enough she could smell his aftershave.

She turned and her knee brushed his.

He leaned forward and picked up his mug, lifting it in a toast. "To the best Christmas ever."

She clinked her mug to his but almost shook her head. No way could this become the best Christmas ever. They sipped their cider, watching each other over the rims. What mouths failed to say, eyes shouted loud and clear. He took her cider mug and set it on the table beside his.

"Blythe, I…"

A languid river lapped at her senses. Time slowed as they leaned closer to each other. With one hand, he cupped her cheek and drew her closer. Their lips touched, brushed.

A tinkle of ornaments. A dog yip.

"Matty, no!" Thane leaped from the sofa and grabbed the tree just before it crashed to the floor. Matty scooted over to her crate and disappeared inside. He made sure the tree was standing straight again. "Silly dog."

"On that note, I'm heading home." Blythe made sure her knees would hold her before she took a step. "Talk about a smashing finale."

He shrugged, his ten-volt smile saddened around the edges. "I'll see you tomorrow?"

# CHAPTER TWELVE

꙰◯◯◯꙰

To go to church or not go to church, that is the question.

Harley jumped up on the bed beside her and planted both front paws on her chest, staring into her eyes, doggy grin firmly in place.

"Ugh, get off you monster. How can a sixty-pound dog weigh a ton?"

He swiped her chin with his tongue and flopped beside her, his sigh saying this was pure heaven. A soft bed, the light of his life and—he lifted her hand with his nose. And petting. He sighed again.

If I get going now, I could go to the early service again and be home in time to hit the computer before anyone calls. Unless it was Thane, of course. He seemed to call at any time and though she tried to not want him to, it wasn't happening. In her case, matter won over mind without a real battle.

Or I could work for awhile, go to regular service and sneak out before Mom insists I come for dinner. I should have invited Thane to family dinner. That would either scare him away or…

"Or nothing. Mind, you must remember that since Amie came into his life, we will be nothing but friends. I cannot, will not, take on little kids. If only they came in older packages, like the girls." She always referred to her two nieces as "the girls." She closed her eyes against the memory, the fear grabbing her like a lion shaking its kill. She rolled over and buried her face in Harley's soft ears. *I can't go through something like that again. I can't.*

Rather than allowing the memories to haunt her, she ordered her dog off the bed, threw back the covers and snagged her robe before heading to the kitchen. Dog out first, fix coffeepot second. As she poured the water in the container, she thought back to the almost kiss the night before. Foiled by a dog and a falling tree. The irony of it made her laugh.

"God, you sure do have a good sense of humor. If this is not the man for me, I should not be kissing him anyway, right?"

The only thing she heard was Harley yipping at the back door.

The music team had already started to play by the time Blythe made it to church. Good thing she'd dressed before she'd hit the computer. The hour and a half had flown by. She found a seat and greeted the older couple sitting in the middle of the pew. She'd known them for years. Closing her eyes, she let the music seep in and her haste leak out. *Thank You, Father that You come to greet me, that*

*You are here, that I am here in spite of all that is piling up on me. Fill me and everyone here with Your Holy Spirit.*

She felt someone take the empty seat on her left, but kept her eyes closed, the better to focus on worship. When the opening chords of "Now is the Time" flowed through her, she opened her eyes and stood along with everyone else. As if pulled by an unseen string, her gaze turned to the person beside her. "Thane."

He smiled down at her, Amie on his left arm. "We made it."

While her heart had been singing worship before, now the praise poured forth, the words and music lifting her higher and higher. Thane came to church. He was standing right beside her. They were singing together. He'd said he only sang in the shower. Then how come his voice turned her insides to jelly and made her want to sing with all her might?

While Amie was restless at first, she soon fell asleep on Thane's lap. The warmth of his shoulder melted into Blythe's, drawing her closer as if being by his side was right where she belonged. After the pastor pronounced the blessing and everyone stood to sing the final hymn, Amie whimpered and rubbed her eyes.

"I'm glad you came." Talk about an understatement.

Thane set Amie on the pew seat and helped her into her jacket. "Me, too. This service is different from what I'm used to but—but this was good."

"Surely this is the Thane we've been hearing about." Blythe's sister held out her hand.

Suzanne, I might have to do you serious bodily harm.

Like I've been raving about him or something. Blythe glanced up to see Thane's eyes sparkling with laughter. "Thane, meet my sister, Suzanne."

"After our phone conversations, I feel like I already know you. How's the ad coming?"

"If you would read it over, I'd appreciate it."

"Gladly." She turned to the couple who'd come up behind her. "Thane, this is our mom and dad, Elsa and Arne."

"We've already met." Thane shook Arne's hand. "I'm glad to meet you, Mrs. Stensrude. And this is my niece, Amie."

"Call me Elsa, please. Has Suzanne invited you to come with us for dinner yet?"

"No, but…" Thane glanced down at Blythe.

"Sorry, but I won't be coming. Mom, I just can't. I have to turn this project in to the company tomorrow morning without fail."

"You're working too hard, dear."

"I've learned my lesson, I'm not booking this much again." There, she'd made the commitment. "I'm really sorry." Sunday was family day in the Stensrude clan and Blythe hated missing it.

Elsa turned to Thane. "You are welcome to come anyway. Amie will have a good time with our granddaughters."

"That's a bit of an imposition, isn't it?"

"Not at all—Mom invites strangers home all the time." Suzanne laughed. "Not that you're a stranger, or *strange,* that is."

Blythe smiled over the glare she sent her sister. *Knock it off.*

"You can follow us home then." Arne touched Thane's arm. "We always have room for two more at our table."

Blythe hugged her family goodbye and walked with Thane out to the parking lot.

"I wish you were coming."

"Me, too. You'll have fun, just don't believe everything you hear."

All afternoon she gritted her teeth and forced thoughts of them all having a good time without her to run away and leave her alone. *Thank You, God, for such intense powers of concentration,* was her heartfelt prayer.

"It's nothing fancy," Elsa said as everyone sat down at the table. "Does that high chair work for Amie?"

"Sure does, thank you." Thane gave Suzanne a smile of relief and thanks when she got the tray to snap in place.

The two nieces sat together on Thane's other side, peeking around him to wave at Amie and make her giggle.

"Alison, Brittany." Suzanne set a bowl of mashed potatoes in the center of the table and took her chair.

"I hope everyone can settle down so we can have grace." Arne looked over his glasses at the two girls.

They grinned back at him and folded their hands.

Out of the corner of his eye, Thane watched Amie copy the other girls, but with an ease that said his sister had taught her some manners. Maybe Linnie hadn't given up praying, either. The thought opened the door to the last time he saw her at the jail. *LynnEllen, God help you, for I no longer can.* The amen brought him back to the table. What if she were telling the truth? He relegated the thought to the impossible bin and let his anger at her tighten his jaw.

"Here, sweetie, how about some potatoes?" Elsa spooned a dab unto Amie's plate, then added gravy. "Here you go, Thane. Help yourself."

When everyone was served, Elsa jumped up. "Oh, the rolls. They're probably burned to a crisp."

"I was supposed to remember the rolls—sorry everyone." Suzanne shook her head. Her husband, Jason, nudged her in the ribs.

"Just because you're not eating bread, you want us all to suffer."

"Right. And if you don't behave you won't get any pie and ice cream, either."

Jason looked across at Thane. "You got to watch these Stensrude women, they'll threaten you with no dessert at the slightest offense."

Suzanne rolled her eyes. "Like you look as if you've missed a lot of desserts."

Thane laughed with the rest of them. He caught Jason's wink, commented on the rolls which, though browned a bit, were still delicious. "Homemade rolls?"

"Mom wouldn't be caught dead serving store-bought." Suzanne smiled at her mother. "Not like her two daughters. That's why we eat Sunday dinner here."

"So we can get a good meal at least once a week." Jason tried to look pathetic, which set his daughters giggling.

*How I wish Blythe were here to enjoy this.* The ten years since his parents died had dimmed his memories of a happy family dinner. But they returned in a swarm. He and his sister teasing each other. His father making his mother laugh. Thane paused, hoping to hear again his mother's laughter, his sister's giggles. But while the pictures came, the sound was too dim to register. Too much sadness buried the song.

"Drink your milk, that's good, Amie." He wiped her face with a napkin.

"She cleaned her plate all up, what a good girl." Elsa patted Amie's hand. "You want some pie and ice cream?"

Amie nodded. "Ice cream."

"Pie, too?"

She shook her head. "Ice cream."

"Looks like she knows her own mind," Arne said as he passed the chair with a stack of plates to carry to the kitchen.

"That she does." *How much do they know about us?* Thane picked up his plate and started to rise, but Elsa shook her head. "You're company, you get to be waited on."

"That's for today, after that you're considered family and we all pitch in." Jason passed by carrying two serving dishes.

After dessert, Amie followed the two girls back to a bedroom that had been turned into a children's sleepover and playroom with a dollhouse, dolls, and all kinds of games and craft things.

"So, how's the house hunting going?" Suzanne asked as she poured him a second cup of coffee.

"I made an offer on one this morning, that's why I was almost late to church."

"Where?" Jason held up his cup.

"Out off Alhambra Valley Road."

"Good for you." Arne picked up the trash to take out, but Jason smiled.

"I'll do that."

"So, did you get the tree up?" Arne led the way into the family room where a larger tree filled the bay window.

"Last night. Blythe brought over her ornaments and tree stand."

"You didn't have any ornaments?" Suzanne turned from adjusting one of the red glass balls on the tree.

"I haven't had a tree since…well, a lot of years. It never seemed necessary and what with getting my business off the ground, I just didn't take the time."

"How sad. Don't you ever go home for Christmas?"

Suzanne's question made Thane sigh. "After my parents died, there's been no home to go back to."

"Leave it to me to stick my foot in my mouth. I'm sorry." Suzanne sat down on the arm of the chair Jason had leaned back in. "Guess we take a lot for granted, don't we?"

"So, tell us about your house." Jason slid his arm around his wife's waist.

Thane told them about the houses he'd looked at and why he chose the one he did. After the discussion, he turned to Suzanne. "I have my ad here, you want to look at it?"

"Of course." She crossed the room to get it and read it standing by Thane. "Will driving be important?"

"Of course."

"Then you need to add that. And English speaking."

He nodded. "Thanks. Anything else?"

"You'll want to run it in both the *Contra Costa Times* and the *San Francisco Chronicle*."

"And the *Oakland Tribune*?"

"Wouldn't hurt."

Amie came and leaned up against his knee.

"You tired, sweetheart?"

She shook her head, but the eyes told the story.

"Think we better get on home. Thank you for the delicious dinner and good visit. You all have a gift of making a stranger feel welcome."

"You're not a stranger, son. You're welcome anytime." Arne stood and shook Thane's hand.

Elsa pressed a package in his hand. "For later."

"That's one thing you'll learn about our family. You never go home without something to snack on later."

"Thank you, all."

Alison helped Amie into her coat. "Here, you take this one." She pressed a tiny baby doll into Amie's hands.

"Thank you, Alison. That was most generous." Thane picked Amie up and with the package under his other arm, headed for the car, the family goodbyes and come again's ringing like the bells of Christmas.

When they returned home, for the first time, in spite of the tree and the scattered toys and Matty yipping her joy, the condo seemed lifeless. He put the sleeping little girl in her bed and tiptoed from the room. Four o'clock. Time to get back to work. *Ah, Blythe, it's a shame we can't work in the same office.*

# CHAPTER THIRTEEN

"Sometimes I hate myself."

Blythe spun her chair around and stared out to the backyard. Harley, tail in the air, was sniffing along the back fence. Dusk blurred the edges of the cedar fencing, turning the Eucalyptus trees into ghosts floating above the fence. Why did she let work come first?

You had to. You made a choice and a commitment. Her little voice made so much sense but... There was always the "but." I missed out. That was the bottom line, she'd missed the family time not just this Sunday but for the last two. She'd missed out on time with Thane.

Unca Dane. How had Amie done with the girls? Alison and Brittany were such fun little girls that Amie most likely had a great time.

Everyone had a great time but me! And Suzanne, if you told him any of our family stories... She shook her head. Time for a tea break.

When she stood up, the yawns caught her and she

stretched her hands over her head to pull out the kinks. Maybe this called for coffee instead of tea. Had she had lunch? Maybe she should call her mother and ask for home delivery.

The food would be good, but she'd missed out on the laughter.

And the love.

She went to the back door and called Harley in. Time to put the pity away and get on with what she needed to be doing.

By the time she turned off the computer that night and organized the CD rack and the sheets of paper, midnight had just chimed on her grandfather clock in the living room. She was ready for the meeting. And exhausted.

Power dressed in a black pinstriped suit, she marched out the door in the morning with all her supplies for her presentation at hand. She drove up to the office building with fifteen minutes to spare and had time to stop in the restroom before entering the offices.

"Hi, Blythe, you all ready?" Gwen, the receptionist, and Blythe had been business acquaintances for the three years she'd handled the company account. "Hey, I like your hair."

"Thanks." Blythe resisted the need to touch it. For once on a presentation day, she didn't have a bad hair day. "They ready?"

Gwen glanced at the clock on her desk. "A couple more minutes. I'll take you back so you can get set up."

"Thanks." Not that she didn't know the way, but an escort was more official.

After everyone settled with their coffee, legal pads and pens, she publicly greeted them and clicked on her infra-red pointer. The presentation lasted twenty-six minutes, but had taken her two weeks to prepare.

At the end she clicked off her screen and motioned for the house lights to be brought back up. "Now I've given each of you a copy of the material so we can begin the discussion." An hour later, she left the building, glowing from the praise heaped upon her and grateful for their desire to continue on to the next step. She wanted to dance and sing out her excitement but that would draw stares and snickers, even in California.

"I did it." She pounded out a three-four time beat on the steering wheel as she started the car. "Thank You, God. You did it." Her praise was a bit late, but heartfelt nonetheless. She'd known from the start the project would take more than she had to give, but the Word said nothing was impossible to those who loved the Lord, so she had proceeded on that promise, and look what happened.

She punched Thane's number into the cell phone and waited. Four rings and an answering machine. That would be a great title for a movie. "Hi, Thane, Blythe here, and I did it. The project I had to finish yesterday was a resounding hit. All for now. Back to the salt mines. Bye."

Next she called Suzanne and got another answering machine.

"Isn't anyone around to celebrate with me today? Not fair!"

Back home she changed into jeans and sweater, ate lunch

from leftovers in the fridge and headed back downstairs, Harley dancing beside her, nosing her hand for more love. She sent an e-mail to her mother, wrote a thank-you letter to the company and dove back into the stack of work left to finish. Eleven shopping days until Christmas and she needed to buy something for Amie and Thane, plus her nieces. Her package to her brother and his family had already been mailed to Alabama.

Sometime later an e-mail popped up from Thane.

"If you want people to return your calls, you should check your machine once in awhile."

"Oops." She clicked the ringer back on and checked the screen. Four messages. Two from Thane, one from Suzanne, including a scolding for being out of touch, and the fourth from someone needing immediate help with a Christmas present.

She regretfully declined the gift project, feeling like a first-class creep. At least it was via the phone and not in person. Sometimes answering machines were a blessing. That sounded good until she got Thane's.

"Oh, for Peter Rabbit's sake." She waited until her time to speak. "If you are screening your calls, you can't complain. My phone is now on and I apologize. Later. Blythe." What had taken him out again?

She caught the next call before the first ring finished. "Blythe's Graphics."

"Hi, this is Kevin and our rates are the lowest they've been in years."

Blythe sighed and shook her head. "Thanks, Kevin, but I'm not in the market for a new mortgage."

"A refi is always helpful."

"No, thanks. And besides, you shouldn't have been able to call me, I've signed on for the no telemarketing calls program."

"Sorry." He hung up abruptly.

"Now, that's why I screen my calls." She clunked the receiver down with more force than necessary.

Back at her computer, she continued clicking through clip art, looking for a design to incorporate in the piece she was working on. When she looked up again, dark obscured the backyard.

When the phone rang, she hesitated, then picked up anyway. "Blythe's Graphics."

"Shouldn't your office be closed now?"

"Hi, Thane. No, my office is never closed." She leaned back in her chair, stretching her neck first to the right, then the left.

"That's a good part of your problem."

"Thanks for the advice." *Right now I do not need a lecture on how to run my business.*

"You said you had something to celebrate."

She thought a moment. This morning seemed so far away. "Oh, the Dunbarry account. My presentation was awesome. They loved it and I walked out of there with the go-ahead for the next step." She slapped her hand on the desk. "I am so pumped."

"That's great. Nice to get a payback for all the work."

"Nice? You call this nice?"

His chuckle made her smile.

"Okay, great then."

"That's better. I would have bought you lunch had you been available."

"I was signing the papers on the house. They accepted my offer."

"The first one?"

"Well, no, I had to up it again, but still—I'm pleased."

"So, which house did you go for?"

"The one on the flat. I'll get a contractor started on that bonus room over the garage as soon as the ink is dry on the final papers."

"You move faster than anyone I've ever known."

"There were two other people making offers."

"Well, congratulations."

"Not quite as close to the freeway but not that far off. I've never owned a house before, just this condo."

She could hear Amie in the background.

"How's she doing?"

"Amie?"

"Yes." What other "she" would I be asking about?

"Better. She had a great time at your mother's yesterday. I tried to call you last night but…"

"I know, the answering machine was on. Why didn't you leave a message?"

"It got late."

"Oh. Well, congrats on your first house."

"I was hoping you would help me decorate it."

"As long as it's not before Christmas."

His chuckle made a warm spot in her middle. "When will you be free?"

"After the first of the year. Or at least back to normal busy."

"Sounds like a plan. Oh, oh, I better go before I regret it. Sweet dreams."

"Bye." She hung up the phone and went to feed Harley. Shame she couldn't ask Thane if he wanted to walk the dogs now. She glanced at the clock. Seven. The park was closed, not that she couldn't get in since only a sign warned people that it closed at dark, not a chain.

She'd just settled in the next morning after her coffee break when, surprise of all surprises, the phone rang.

He didn't wait for her business greeting. "Blythe, I have a serious problem."

She could tell by his tone he wasn't kidding. "What's up?"

"I told you I was taking time off to get things settled?"

"Right?" Why did she have a not good feeling in her stomach?

"I just got a call from Cymex and they are desperate. They insist that I come. I have to go into the city for this, no choice. Would you please come watch Amie for about four hours? I should be back by two, three at the latest."

Blythe knew he'd not had time to find a local sitter yet. And Suzanne was already gone shopping. What about her mother? Fear set her heart to hammering. She looked at her calendar.

"What do you say? Please, I'm begging you."

"You promise you'll be back on time. I have a very important meeting at five."

"I promise."

"You could bring her here." She glanced around her office. "No, where her toys and things are will be better. But Thane Davidson, you'll owe me big-time for this one." *You have no idea how big…*

"Thank you. How soon can you get here?"

"Give me half an hour." She hung up the phone and turned off her computer. So much for getting that project done today. Surely if Amie took a nap, she could work on something else. She made sure her notes and the manila envelope she'd need for her meeting were in her briefcase, gathered up a few other things, bade Harley behave and out the door she went. *You can do this,* she ordered herself. *It's just for a couple of hours. Surely nothing can happen in that short a time. You can do this.*

He met her at the door, Amie already crying in his arms, two bulging briefcases at his feet.

"Hi, sorry, I tried to warn her."

"Not a good thing. Just leave, she'll settle down." *This is one time I hope I don't have to eat my words.* She reached for Amie but the little girl arched her back and screamed.

"No, want Unca Dane."

Thane set her down. "I'm sorry, Amie, but I have to go. Blythe will be here. You be good and I'll bring you a present."

Amie melted down into a bundle on the floor, weeping as if her heart was broken beyond mending.

Thane gave Blythe a look of total confusion and despair. "I've not left her since I picked her up at Lynn-Ellen's neighbors."

"I know. Go." When the door shut behind him, she knelt by the sobbing child.

"Mommy, I—hic—want—my mommy."

The words tore at Blythe's heart. "Of course you want your mommy but she can't come here. Shall we go sit on the sofa and I'll read you a story?"

"Noooo—hic—Mommy. Unca Dane." The sobbing continued with Blythe sitting on the floor, patting Amie's shoulder and rubbing comfort circles on her back.

How long could this child cry?

Should I put her to bed? Pick her up whether she wants me to or not and hold her on the sofa? Run screaming myself?

Humming a soft tune, she kept up the patting and moving her fingers lightly over Amie's back. Slowly the sobs lessened to sniffs and hiccups. Matty came out of her crate and sat beside Blythe, so she used one hand to comfort the dog. Matty leaned against her and sighed.

"Good girl." Blythe wasn't sure if she meant the dog or the little girl. What would it be like to have your mother disappear like that and a man you hardly know dismantle your home, load you in a car and drive to the end of nowhere. Poor little one. Lord, I don't know what to do here, other than what I'm doing. If You have any suggestions, could You please send them on?

Matty crawled up in her cross-legged lap and reached up to lick her chin.

"Now Harley is going to know I was here and he'll get

all excited. Wish I could have taken the two of you to my house." *What I really wish is that I was home in my house and working away.*

"You want some juice, Amie?

She shook her head.

"Okay, then Matty and I'll have some."

"Bad doggy."

"No, Matty is a good dog." Blythe set the dog aside and stood, her knees creaking, her feet sending screaming shards of pain up her legs. She closed her eyes and stood in one place, waiting for the needles to go away.

When she returned, setting a half-filled sippy cup and her own glass of apple juice on the table, Amie had rolled over and lay staring at the ceiling. Green marker pen now decorated the front of her T-shirt and the carpet—and her face.

*I should have known better than to leave you alone.* "Oh, boy, guess no one's taught you to only draw on paper." Blythe scooped up the child and carried her to the bathroom. Setting her on the counter, she waited until the water warmed before soaking a washcloth. "Next time you color on paper." It took soap and several scrubbings to clean Amie's face, making her whimper. "While I have you here, we should probably brush your hair, too." *Looks like Unca Dane has a problem with barrettes and ribbons and such, let alone getting the snarls out.* In spite of the lack of cooperation, Blythe got the child cleaned, dressed and set back in the bathroom to comb her hair. First she looked in the cabinet to see if there was some spray to take out the tangles. No such luck. Okay, water would help.

Amie alternated wailing and scowling all the way

through. But when Blythe finished, she turned her around to look in the mirror. "See how pretty you look. Amie looks so nice, all clean and pretty again."

Other than the scowl.

Blythe set Amie on the floor with a book and went for the cleaning supplies. She sprayed the green marks, scrubbed and patted dry and scrubbed some more. If that didn't do it, he'd have to call in the carpet cleaners.

Lunch of grilled cheese sandwiches ended up on the floor, making Matty very happy. The faithful sippy cup was the only thing that saved the juice. Only drops came out, not a deluge. Good thing it wasn't orange or grape juice.

She put Amie down for a nap, ignoring the cries "I want my mommy." I want your mommy, too, but not for the same reason. Why couldn't she put you ahead of the drugs? You poor, poor, baby. She sat on the edge of the bed, patting Amie's back and crooning until she finally dropped off to sleep.

One-thirty and no word from Thane. She cleaned up the kitchen, put away the things in the bathroom. One-forty-five. No Thane.

The clock inched past two, then two-thirty.

"For crying out loud, he has a cell phone, why doesn't he call?"

Matty looked at her, looked at the door and whined.

"Sorry, girl, you're going to have to hold it."

Amie woke up, cranky and whiny.

"Sorry, child, but the dog needs to go out. Let's get your jacket on."

"No."

"Don't you know any word but no?" She stuffed Amie's arms in the sleeves and pulled the jacket in place. "Here we go. Where's the leash?" Where would Thane keep the leash? She checked the coat closet and the cabinet where the cleaning supplies were kept. "For crying out loud, Thane, where do you keep the leash?"

"In der." Amie pointed to a drawer in the pantry.

Voilà, a leash. "Thank you, Amie, what an observant little girl you are." Blythe snapped the leash on a dancing Matty and, taking the little girl by the hand, headed out the door. What if it locked? No key. Matty whined, straining at the leash. Blythe closed her eyes, the better to think. Okay, if someone breaks in while we're gone, I will not be held responsible. She set the dead bolt out, rested the door against it and headed for the elevator.

Three-fifteen, but who was counting? It would take her half an hour to get to her meeting.

Three-thirty and they were back in the condo, no break-ins or things missing. She hung up Amie's jacket, put away the leash and took three deep breaths to calm herself. If she didn't hear from him by four, she'd have to call and cancel. Hopefully they could reschedule for sometime later this week. Four hours, he said. I know there's probably some emergency but he could at least call.

Her client was less than happy. "It wouldn't be a problem usually, Blythe, but I'm going out of town early tomorrow and I needed to send this off with the rest of the package—before I leave."

"Is there someplace we can meet tonight? Could I take it by your house?"

# Get 2 Books FREE!

## Steeple Hill Books,
### publisher of inspirational romance fiction, presents

*Love Inspired*

A series of contemporary love stories that will lift your spirits and reinforce important lessons about life, faith and love!

**FREE BOOKS!**
Get two free books by best-selling, inspirational authors!

**FREE GIFT!**
Get an exciting surprise gift absolutely free!

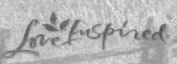

# HOW TO GET YOUR
# 2 FREE BOOKS AND FREE GIFT

1. Peel off the 2 FREE BOOKS sticker from the front cover. Place it in the space provided at right. This automatically entitles you to receive two free books and an exciting surprise gift.

2. Send back this card and you'll get 2 Love Inspired® books. These books have a combined cover price of $9.98 in the U.S. and $11.98 in Canada, but they are yours to keep absolutely FREE!

3. There's <u>no</u> catch. You're under <u>no</u> obligation to buy anything. We charge nothing – ZERO – for your first shipment. And you don't have to make any minimum number of purchases – not even one!

4. We call this line Love Inspired because each month you'll receive books that are filled with joy, faith and traditional values. The stories will lift your spirits and gladden your heart! You'll like the convenience of getting them delivered to your home well before they are in stores. And you'll love our discount prices, too!

5. We hope that after receiving your free books you'll want to remain a subscriber. But the choice is yours – to continue or cancel, anytime at all! So why not take us up on our invitation, with no risk of any kind. You'll be glad you did!

6. And remember…we'll send you a surprise gift ABSOLUTELY FREE just for giving Love Inspired novels a try!

**Steeple Hill®**

® and TM are trademarks owned and used by the trademark owner and/or its licensee.

Order online at:
www.LoveInspiredBooks.com

## SPECIAL FREE GIFT!

We'll send you a fabulous surprise gift, absolutely FREE, simply for accepting our no-risk offer!

©1997 STEEPLE HILL BOOKS

# Books FREE!

DETACH AND MAIL CARD TODAY!

## HURRY!
### Return this card promptly to get
### 2 FREE books
### and a FREE gift!

*Love Inspired*

**YES,** please send me the 2 FREE *Love Inspired* books and FREE gift for which I qualify. I understand that I am under no obligation to purchase anything further, as explained on the opposite page.

affix
free
books
sticker
here

313 IDL EE4E                113 IDL EE4Q

|  |
|--|
| FIRST NAME |

|  |
|--|
| LAST NAME |

|  |
|--|
| ADDRESS |

| APT.# | CITY |
|--|--|

| STATE/PROV. | ZIP/POSTAL CODE |
|--|--|

(LI-LA-06)

Offer limited to one per household and not valid to current Love Inspired® subscribers. All orders subject to approval. Credit or debit balances in a customer's account(s) may be offset by any other outstanding balance owed by or to the customer. Please allow 4 to 6 weeks for delivery.

## Steeple Hill Reader Service™—Here's How It Works:

Accepting your 2 free books and gift places you under no obligation to buy anything. You may keep the books and gift and return the shipping statement marked "cancel." If you do not cancel, about a month later we will send you 4 additional books and bill you just $3.99 each in the U.S., or $4.74 each in Canada, plus 25¢ shipping & handling per book and applicable taxes if any.* That's the complete price, and — compared to cover prices of $4.99 each in the U.S. and $5.99 each in Canada — it's quite a bargain! You may cancel at any time, but if you choose to continue, every month we'll send you 4 more books, which you may either purchase at the discount price...or return to us and cancel your subscription.

*Terms and prices subject to change without notice. Sales tax applicable in N.Y.
Canadian residents will be charged applicable provincial taxes and GST.

"Let me think. I'll be here until six if you can make it by then."

If I had a car seat, I could take Amie with me. No car seat, no drive. "I'll try to make that." Surely Thane would be back by then.

Amie dragged out her blankie and Pooh Bear, sniffing again and looking about to cry. "Unca Dane."

"I know. He'll be back soon."

"Crackers, chips."

"You're hungry?" Of course you are, you didn't eat any lunch." She checked the cupboards. No crackers, no chips. He'd not really done much shopping yet. "Cheese?"

"No, no cheese." She threw herself on the sofa, crying again.

"Bread and peanut butter."

"Chips."

I can't do this. Blythe sat down on the sofa. "Amie, there are no chips here, so if you are hungry I will fix you another sandwich."

"Mommy, Mommy." The cries grew louder.

Blythe picked up the child, set her in her lap, along with blankie and Pooh Bear, and rocked. It would have been easier with a real rocking chair but this would have to do.

Darkness fell early but she kept on rocking.

She glanced at her watch when she heard Thane's key in the lock. Five-fifteen. She could still make it.

"I'm sorry, the bridge was backed up and my cell phone wouldn't work."

"Fine." She handed him the child, grabbed her purse and tore out the door.

"Where are you going?"

She paused at the elevator, then threw over her shoulder. "I have to deliver something."

"I'll take you."

"No." She hit the exit door running and continued so to the bottom. Four flights wasn't that bad. A drum started up in her temples. *If I never have an afternoon like this one again, it will be too soon.*

# CHAPTER FOURTEEN

The picture in his mind remained.

With the child in bed, asleep, Thane finally took time to close his eyes. His recliner kicked back, *Pachelbel's Canon* on the music system and Matty by his side, he let the scene return in full color. Blythe sitting on the couch with Amie, blankie and all, on her lap, held close. Would that he could come home to that scene every day.

She cares for me, I know she does. You can't have attraction as strong as we have without caring. At least I can't and I don't think she can, either. But—there always had to be a but. But she continually shied away from talk of children. But she had cared for Amie all afternoon and the house was all of a piece when he got home.

However, that was anger pure and simple that he saw on her face as she ran out the door. She'd said she had a meeting at five. He'd tried his best to get back, but when you are stuck in the middle of the Bay Bridge with a major accident ahead, there is nothing you can do but

wait. And want to kill your cell phone that, for some in-
explicable reason known only to cell phones, died. He
almost got out of his car to ask someone else to call her
for him. He should have. Or, plan B, he could have left
her the car seat, not that taking Amie to a business meeting would have worked either, but she would have had
more options.

He rested his glass of milk on his chest and let the
music flow over him. Getting sleepier by the moment, he
drained the glass and set it on the floor. At least he'd been
successful at Cymex. He glanced at the clock. Eight-
thirty. Time to start trying to reach Blythe. To explain
what all had happened—and find out if she made it to her
appointment.

*I have to tell him that I can't see him anymore.* Blythe
heaved a sigh that ripped from the soles of her feet and
blew out strong enough that Harley raised his head, ears
cocked. "You don't need to worry, there's nothing outside."

He laid back down, soulful gaze still on her.

*Amie is a sweet child. Liar.* She's about as sweet as
half-ripe lemons. Interesting, needy, cute, but not sweet.
*All right, so start again. Amie needs a mother, misses her
mommy something dreadful. She has an uncle who will
lay down his life for her.*

*Why couldn't she be a couple of years older? Out of
the danger stage.*

"I need to call Thane and apologize for my hasty flight.
But I made it and that's all that counts." *No, that's not all
that counts. The people in your life are far more impor-*

tant than getting the work done. Once a commitment is made, you live up to it.

He'll probably have his answering machine on. Silly, he's not the one screening his calls. If psychiatrists got a hold of me and learned of the voices arguing in my head, they'd use me as an example of multiple personalities for sure. At least her headache had quit.

And it wasn't really Thane's fault he was late. The bridges could be snarled for hours at a time. She'd heard about the accident on the evening news, a bad one, two dead, multiple vehicles.

So, call him.

He should call me. Oh, don't hide in the past. Just call him and get this sorted out.

Could they be friends? Just friends. Anytime she heard a friend say that about one of the opposite sex, she knew love was on the way. Or had already arrived. Or was over. Scary thought.

She picked up the phone to dial. No dial tone.

"Hello?" Talk about a familiar voice.

"Thane? I never even dialed. I was calling you."

"Well, I dialed but it never rang." Their chuckles danced together over the wires. "So, did you…"

"Thane, I…" They stopped since they were talking at the same time.

"Okay, ladies first."

"I'm sorry I yelled at you like that."

"Forgiven. Did you make your delivery?"

"Yes, just. He'd have been in real trouble if he'd not gotten it today. A lot of other things depended on it."

"I'm so sorry to cause you problems like that. Can you forgive me?"

"Forgiven. Did you get the emergency taken care of?" Tell him. Go away.

"Yes, and I was so excited, I was on my way home in plenty of time and then the bridge locked up." Even the silence felt good. "How did you and Amie do?"

"I'd say she could be called a strong-willed child."

"Like her mother."

"Anyone else in the family come to mind?" She waited through a not so comfortable silence.

He sighed. "Me?"

"If the shoe fits...?"

"I've had to be strong-willed enough for both of us or LynnEllen would not be alive now. And where would I be in the business world if I were a wimp?"

A note of testiness on his part made her smile. "Besides, it takes one to know one?"

His chuckle eased the tension. "I wasn't the one who skipped the traditional and delicious family Sunday dinner to work."

'But I'll bet you've missed more than a few."

"Touché. So, back to my question regarding Amie. Did she cry all the time I was gone?"

"A good part of it. She's one observant little girl though. Matty had to go out, so I was looking for the leash and she showed me where it was."

"Good. I should have left you a key—and the car seat in case of emergencies."

The word emergencies sucked the joy right out of the

conversation for her. "Thane, I have something very important to tell you."

"Uh, oh, be right back."

Blythe waited. She could hear Amie crying in the background.

Thane picked up the phone again. " I gotta go. She's having nightmares a lot, poor baby."

"Good night, then." After hanging up the phone, Blythe sat curled in her favorite chair. What was the matter with her? She'd wanted to throw her clothes back on and go help him. Was there a chance she could keep a small child safe? Would love be enough?

The next afternoon she received an e-mail. "Sorry for the interruption last night. I have found a sitter. Can we go to dinner tomorrow night? Just the two of us."

She checked her calendar and hit Reply. "Yes, what time and where?"

"Benjamin's. I'll pick you up at seven."

"Good, I'm looking forward to it." She sat back. Interesting that he used e-mail rather than the phone. And it worked. She went back to moving clip art around to get the right effect.

Deep purple slacks, violet silk blouse and dangley earrings of brilliantly hued parrots. A matching pendant hung from a short chain. She checked out her reflection in the full length mirror. Harley barked. Thane was right on time.

"Hi." She opened the door and invited him in. "Let me

get Harley his chew and we'll be on our way. Harley, down, you know better than that."

Thane patted the dog, then gave her a funny look.

"What?"

"I have news, you decide if it is good or bad."

She lifted her coat off the hanger in the closet. "What is it?"

"The sitter bailed."

"So…?"

"So we have Amie and we'll go somewhere child friendly." His gaze implored her to understand. "You look lovely." He stepped back out to wave to Amie in the car seat.

What could she say? No? "Why didn't you call me?"

"I just wanted to see you and this seemed the only way." He checked on his charge again.

"You go on out there, I'll be out in a minute."

"Okay, thanks."

Guess the serious talking will wait for another time. She fetched Harley's treat and tossed it down the hallway. His scrabbling nails on the hardwood floor as he chased the dried pig's ear made her smile. She shrugged into her coat and locked the door behind her.

They waited only a few minutes at Marie Calender's, which was a miracle in itself.

"What a cutie you have there," the waitress said as she led them to a table. "You want a high chair or a booster seat?"

"Thanks, we'll take a high chair." Thane set Amie down in one of the wooden chairs. "You wait while we get our coats off." He laid his jacket across the empty chair and helped Blythe out of hers. "Amie, I said, sit still, you can't stand in the chair." Amie turned around, hanging on to the back and grinned at the people behind them.

Thane plopped her back down. "I said, sit still."

Blythe noted the tension in his jaw. This little one was going to lead him on a merry chase. Blythe pulled out her chair and sat down.

"Here you go." The waitress set the high chair in place.

Thane put Amie in the chair and scooted it up to the table, then took his own chair. "Sorry. I didn't know this was going to turn into a circus."

"What can I get you folks to drink?" the waitress asked.

"Milk for her and…" Thane inclined his head toward his niece.

"Juice," Amie stated.

"Iced tea for me," Blythe told the waitress.

"I'll take the same. And juice for Amie."

Blythe hid her smile.

"Would you like crayons for the little girl?" the waitress asked before leaving to get their drinks.

"Please."

"You have crackers also?" Blythe asked.

"Be right back."

The crackers and crayons both arrived, along with the drinks. Thane handed Amie a crayon and a place mat to color on.

"Cackers, please."

He ripped one pack open and handed her a saltine. "There's a good girl."

The waitress returned, giving Thane an extra big smile. "Now, can I take your orders?" She turned to Blythe first.

"I'll have the chicken with artichoke hearts, salad with ranch dressing and corn bread."

"You don't want the salad bar?"

"No thank you, just the dinner salad."

"And you, sir?"

"I'll have the steak, medium, baked potato and the house salad also." He glanced at Amie, who was carefully shredding the cracker on the floor. He took another calming breath. "And she'll have chicken fingers."

"Hamburger." Amie picked up the second cracker, took a bite and watched the broken bits float to the carpet.

"Will she want fries with that?"

"Amie, do you want French fries?"

"Yes."

"So, how was your day?" His voice sounded more than a little strained.

Blythe smiled at him, as much to comfort as to please. "Good. I got a lot done and I found a B and B for Mom and Dad. Suzanne and I are giving them a weekend in the Gold Country for their Christmas gift." The poor man had thought having Amie along wouldn't be a problem. He's learning.

"They'll enjoy that." He took the crayon out of Amie's mouth. "I should have brought the sippy cup, shouldn't I?"

Blythe nodded. "It would be a good idea. And a couple of small toys. Suzanne used to bring a baggy of Cheerios, too."

Their salads arrived. "Would you like pepper with that?"

"No, thanks." Blythe smiled up at the woman.

"Pepper."

Thane grinned. "She's right, I want pepper." He turned to Amie. "You're a parrot."

"She's sure a live wire." The waitress smiled and cranked the pepper grinder over Thane's salad.

Blythe glanced down at the mess on the floor and shuddered.

The waitress stopped at the high chair. "Where did you get that cute shirt?" She poked Amie on the shoulder.

"My aunt Sandy gibbed it to me."

"Well, you're a pretty lucky girl to have such a nice aunt."

Thane froze, then stared at Amie. "When did you see your aunt Sandy?"

Amie appeared to be thinking deeply. "Afore you came to me." She reached for a piece of Thane's salad.

Blythe watched Thane's face. Something was going on here.

The waitress set the dinner plates in front of them. "Here you go."

Blythe reached over and tied a paper bib around Amie's neck. "You wait, that might be hot."

"Not really, we're careful about that. Can I get you anything else?"

"I don't think so. Thank you."

Thane leaned over and cut Amie's hamburger patty into bite-size pieces. "Now you chew." He groaned and clamped his hand over his pocket. "The phone." He checked the display. "I need to take this call. Excuse me." He rose and strode from the room, the cell phone clamped to his ear.

"Unca Dane." Amie cranked her head around to watch him leave.

"He'll be right back." Please don't pitch a fit now. Let's just get this dinner over with. Blythe took up her fork. "Use your fork, Amie."

Amie picked up her fork, stabbed one of the pieces and put it in her mouth.

"Good girl." Blythe cut her corn bread in half and spread the honey butter on both sides to melt in. "You want some corn bread?"

"No." Amie speared a French fry but when her fork couldn't pick it up, she used her fingers.

Blythe ignored her and ate part of her own dinner.

"Unca Dane come back?"

"Soon. Or his dinner will get cold."

"Cold."

Blythe smiled at the little girl. "You're a funny one, you know that?" She cut a bite of her corn bread. But before it could reach her mouth, she heard a gagging sound.

"Amie! Spit it out." She held her hand in front of Amie's mouth but nothing came out.

Amie coughed and gagged, arms flailing.

*Please, God, no, not again.* Blythe jumped to her feet, grabbed Amie and fisted her hands just above the little girl's navel, beginning to move in the method she'd prayed never to have to use. *Please, God, not again.*

# CHAPTER FIFTEEN

❦

The piece of ground beef hit the floor.

Amie coughed, sucked in a huge breath of air and let out a scream that brought half the wait staff running.

Blythe hugged her close, "You're okay now, it's okay, Amie."

"What happened?" The man behind them stood by her side.

"She choked on a bite of her food. She's fine now."

Thane pushed his way to their table. "What happened?"

Blythe ignored the tears streaming down her cheeks. "She choked on a piece of food."

"Unca Dane." Still sobbing and coughing, Amie reached out and he took her in his arms.

"Hush, baby, you're all right now."

"Can we go?" I can't stay here one more minute.

"Of course, if you want."

"Can I get you anything?" Their waitress hovered at their table, the manager right behind her.

"Yes, the check. I need to get my girls home." Thane bundled Amie into her jacket, murmuring comfort.

Blythe kept herself rigid, fighting to keep from screaming. Be polite. Don't make a scene. She wanted to clap her hands over her ears, block out Amie's sobs now reduced to hiccups, the people around them settling back into their seats.

"There will be no charge. If you need anything, please let me know." The manager kept his voice low.

"Thank you, we're fine now. It wasn't your fault." Thane settled Amie on his arm and motioned for Blythe to precede him.

Once he had Amie in her car seat, he climbed in the driver's side. Blythe had both arms locked around her upper body. "Blythe, what is it?"

"Please, just take me home."

"Of course, but I…"

"*Now.* I want to go home." She swallowed hard to force the gagging back down. The shaking that had begun in the restaurant had increased to shudders.

Thane put a hand on her shoulder, but she turned away. "Blythe, darling, what is it? Amie is all right."

Blythe stared out the windshield. She couldn't be trusted with small children. If only she could disappear. Drive faster, Thane. Please drive faster. As soon he stopped the truck in her driveway, she leaped from the vehicle and ran to the house.

"Blythe."

"No, no." Her fingers shook so it took three tries to get the key in. She turned it, flung open the door and staggered inside. She could hear Amie screaming for her uncle. He was right behind her. "You go to her. She needs you." She shut the door in his face, ran to the bathroom and threw up in the commode.

For some time she sat crumpled on the floor, until the cold of the tile beneath her seeped through her coat. Tears flowed unchecked. Harley sat beside her, his whimpers ignored. Finally he raised his muzzle and lifted a mournful howl. Blythe wrapped her arms around his neck and cried into his fur.

When she finally raised her face, he licked her tears away, his tongue soft as rose petals. She could hear the phone ringing and Thane calling her to pick up. She ignored the ringing. Ignored the hole his voice tore in her heart. When she crawled into bed, Harley beside her, she didn't quit shivering for what seemed like forever. Sometimes loving meant you had to let go. He didn't deserve to be saddled with an emotional cripple like her. Slowly she released her hand and lay with it palm up, so he could fly free.

"Blythe, honey." Elsa sat on her daughter's bed.

"Mom, what are you doing here?" Blythe gazed around at her bedroom full of sunlight. She jerked fully awake. "Amie, is she all right?"

"Thane called us. Amie is fine. He was frantic."

"Oh." Blythe flopped back on her pillows. "Where's Harley?"

"Your dad has him out from the backyard."

"Oh." She blinked, as if from far away, trying to see

what time it was. She glanced down to see that she was still dressed in silk slacks and blouse. "How come you're here?" Nothing was making sense. Her mind refused to leave the land of deep stupor. A shroud of blackness hovered at the edges.

"Thane called us. He said you won't answer your phone."

Blythe nodded. "I don't want to see him." A shudder swept from head to foot.

"But why?"

"I let Amie die. No, no." She clenched her eyes shut. She reared up, fear and fury warring for supremacy. "Can't you see! It was just like Robert. Choking, getting blue. He died, don't you remember? It happened again. I can't be trusted with little children. I let them die." She could hear herself screaming, but like catching smoke, she couldn't make it stop. She clutched her mother's shoulders, hiding in her embrace.

"But Blythe, dearest Blythe, your little brother didn't die, and neither did Amie."

"Yes, they did, I saw them last night. Blue—and—and dead." Another shudder followed the tears. "Dead, they were dead."

Her mother held her close, stroking her head, just as if she held a little girl in her arms. "Where did you see them?"

"Last night…" Blythe pulled back enough to stare into her mother's eyes. Elsa shook her head, gentle, small movements, not even blinking. "Last night…" The words came one at a time as if dredged up from some horrendous pit. "Last—night—in a dream. I haven't had that dream for a long time. Robert lying dead. And now there was Amie, too. All my fault." Blythe gazed around her room, wonder filling her eyes. "But Mom, Robert lives in Alabama. Thane took Amie home. She coughed and the hamburger came out."

"Yes."

"But I've been so afraid."

"I'm so sorry, Blythe, you never told me about the nightmares."

"I never told anyone. Suzanne used to wake me up." Blythe felt like she was walking in a dream world, but this time—this time the sun was coming up. The night fears, the black shroud, were banished by the light.

"I need to call Thane."

"You won't have to call loud, he's in the living room."

"I can't let him see me like this."

"Yes, you can." Thane filled the doorway, leaning nonchalantly against the frame.

But Blythe could see the tension in his jawline, the furrow between his thick brows.

"Where's Amie?"

"At Suzanne's."

"I think I'll leave the two of you alone." Elsa kissed her daughter on the forehead and left the room.

"I need a shower." She felt like hiding under the covers. "How much did you hear?"

"All of it. You'll have to forgive me for eavesdropping but when you screamed—I—I couldn't stay away." He crossed the room, one slow step at a time, holding her gaze with eyes that burned with—with what?

Ah, she recognized the look. Love, only love, could look like that. She patted the bed beside her. After all, she was fully dressed, even though rumpled as if she'd slept in her clothes—which she had. "I bet I have bed head." She brushed her fingers back through her hair.

"You look beautiful to me." He sat down and took her hand in his. "I had no idea."

"The scary thing is that I didn't, either. How could fear blind me so?"

"I don't know, but God made us incredibly complex creatures. No wonder he says to cast out fear." He lifted her hand, inch by inch, his gaze locked on hers, then kissed the palm. "I love you, Blythe Stensrude."

Tears blurred the sight of him. Her palm felt on fire, burned clean. "I…" She cleared her throat and tried again. "Give me time, all right. I think what I feel is the beginning of love but I have to make sure."

"I'm in no hurry. You can have five minutes." He raised her watch, grinning at her over his arm.

"Thane." She sniffed back tears that kept threatening to overflow.

He turned her hand over and kissed her knuckles. "Truly, take your time. I have all the time in the world."

Amie walked between them, holding on to each of their hands, as they climbed the broad concrete steps to the church. The beauty of "Oh Come, Oh Come, Emmanuel" flowed out the open doors, inviting them and the crowd in to celebrate with the singing Christmas Tree.

"Do the tree sing?" Amie asked.

Thane looked down and scooped her up in his arms. "Guess we'll have to see."

"Merry Christmas," the usher greeted them and handed them a program.

Once seated and studying the program, Thane asked, "This was one of your projects, right?"

"Right."

"You do good work."

"Thank you."

"Joy to the World" broke forth and the lights dimmed. The choir entered, each member holding a candle, and made their way to the tree-shaped risers to the right of the stage.

"Pretty." Amie looked to Blythe.

"It is." Pretty was far too plain a word for the scene unfolding. Thank You, Father, for the gift of Your son and for being here, for the three of us.

Amie stared wide-eyed when Mary rode down the center aisle on a donkey, and shot Thane a look of awe at the sheep with the shepherds. The angels burst forth with glorias from all around them, one hovering above the manger scene.

Blythe's heart swelled with joy as Joseph held baby Jesus up for all the congregation to see and said the words of scripture. "And his name shall be called Jesus." The choir burst into "Mary had a Baby Named Jesus," the rhythm setting her feet to tapping.

After the wise men departed, the lights changed and the pastor turned to smile at the congregation. "And he came that we might have life, and have it abundantly. Love came to earth that we might be set free from sin, free from fear. All we need to do is accept Jesus into our hearts so that we can live with him forever. I invite you to come this night and do just that."

A violin sang, joined by a piano and a soprano voiced the haunting words of "Lo, How a Rose E'er Blooming." The notes drifted off into the hush. No one stirred.

A child started, "Jesus loves me this I know." Another joined on the second line and the choir director turned and motioned them all to join in. At the finish, the lights went out, but for the single candle burning bright in the center of the stage.

A deep male voice echoed through the darkness. "In him was life and the life was the light of men. And the light shines in the darkness and the darkness does not put it out. A blessed Christmas to you all. Amen."

Even Amie was quiet on the way back to Thane's condo, as if absorbing what she had seen. Thane reached across the console and took Blythe's hand. She covered them with her other.

Softly playing Christmas carols greeted them as they entered the condo. Thane took their coats. "Amie, you can turn on the tree lights."

As if honored, the little girl picked up the switch box and clicked it. The twinkle lights turned the dark tree into life, like the candle on the stage. "Ooh, pretty."

Thane lit the three fat candles in a row in the long, narrow arrangement of greens and red plaid bows on the coffee table. The fragrance of evergreens, winterberry candles and spiced apple cider mingled, another reminder of the season.

Blythe let the dogs out of their crates and settled them at her feet.

Thane served cups of cider to the three of them, making sure that Amie knelt by the coffee table to drink hers. "Merry Christmas." He touched his cup to Blythe's, then Amie's. The little girl giggled.

"Mewwy Chrimas."

A bit later, after putting Amie to bed, Blythe sat next to Thane on the sofa, her feet drawn up under her. "I have…"

He said at the same time. "I have…"

They chuckled together, as Thane slid his arm around her shoulders.

"You first." She waited.

"I made a rather interesting decision."

"Yes."

"Do you remember when the waitress asked Amie where she got her shirt and she said her aunt Sandy 'gibbed' it to her?"

"Sort of."

"Well, it set me to thinking. One of LynnEllen's parole stipulations was that she could have no contact with former druggy friends. I have a feeling that was the secret she was keeping. Linnie wasn't lying when she said the stash wasn't hers. She knew nothing about it, but she had given Sandy a ride somewhere and Sandy left her a gift—the baggy of crack. The evidence that put her away."

"What will you do?"

"Everything I can to get her out of there. But first tell her I believe her."

Blythe fought tears, the tears that had floated so near

the surface all night. "That's wonderful. Oh, Thane, I'm so proud of you."

"It's all your fault, you know."

"My fault?" She turned to watch his face.

"Well, I figured if you could let go of fear, I could let go of judgment. I've forgiven my sister and now I just have to let her know."

Blythe quit fighting the tears. Harley whimpered at her feet, then stood and laid his head on her knees. "It's okay, Harley. These are good tears." She took in a deep breath. "Now is it my turn?"

"I guess."

"I love you, Thane Davidson. With all my heart and for all time." She place a hand on his cheek and brought his head down for the kiss they'd waited so long to share.

"Will you marry me?" He moved his head only enough to whisper the words against her lips.

"In a heartbeat. But it will take at least a couple of weeks to put a wedding together."

"That long?" He kissed her again. "I will always remember this as the best Christmas ever."

"Me, too. And it's not even Christmas yet."

Harley whined. Matty whimpered. As if they planned it, the two bassets bounded onto the sofa and into the laps of those they loved. This night truly was the most special time of the year.

* * * * *

# DISCUSSION QUESTIONS

*The Most Wonderful Time of the Year*

1. Fictional characters often function as a mirror for a reader, reflecting back characteristics we recognize in ourselves. Which character is most like you? What personality traits of Blythe and Thane spoke to you?

2. Both Blythe and Thane developed as individuals during the course of the story. How did your favorite character grow in the story? How did this development enable them to fall in love?

3. Blythe and Thane love their bassets very much, and in fact meet through their dogs. How has your pet (or how have your pets) influenced your life?

4. Thane found it difficult to deal with his sister's incarceration, and Blythe faced similar trouble dealing with his niece. What would you have done in these situations? What lessons did each character learn about himself/herself?

# 'TWAS THE WEEK
# BEFORE CHRISTMAS

## Lenora Worth

❧ ❧ ❧

To Sandy Smith,
a great friend and a faithful reader!

# CHAPTER ONE

Everything here is old.

Elise Melancon stood staring out at the bright red cardinals fighting over birdseed in the wintry courtyard of her grandmother's gracious home and wondered why she'd agreed to meet her parents here at *Belle Terre* for her two-week Christmas vacation.

She could have been skiing in Vail, or traveling around Europe with friends. Instead, at her mother's—well, more like her grandmother's—insistence, Elise had decided to spend the entire holiday season with the family down in the southern most region of Louisiana.

But why had *Grand-mère* insisted? Elise wondered as she studied the bright red velveteen Christmas bows adorning the huge columns surrounding the house on all sides. And what was Elise to do with herself here in the bayous and swamps of south Louisiana for two whole weeks? Elise knew there would be the obligatory duties to keep her busy—the open-house Christmas gatherings, the usual round of parties and holiday get-togethers, even the annual bonfire on the river. But those were traditions that meant more to her parents and her grandmother than they did to Elise. *Grand-mère* knew this about Elise, knew that being twenty-five and on the cusp of life meant more than just tradition. Didn't it?

Elise thought about her life back in Shreveport. She had gone right out of college to a handpicked job as communications director for Melancon Oil and Gas. Although there was no one serious in her life, she dated interesting men and she had a great group of friends to hang around with. She'd even found a good church home, per her formidable grandmother's parting instructions years ago when Elise and her parents had moved to Shreveport.

But was there more out there?

Elise glanced around the quiet halls of her grandmother's home, her gaze taking in the large Douglas fir centered in the marble-floored entrance hall, its branches decorated with all her grandmother's favorite antique Victorian ornaments. The whole house glowed with all the frills of the holidays—holly branches draped across the Hepplewhite sideboard in the dining room, magnolia leaves glistening across the Sheraton secretary in the front parlor, and frosted pinecones and cinnamon-scented candles centered on the long Duncan Phyfe dining table in the formal dining room.

This house had been in the Melancon family for generations. Built in 1845, *Belle Terre*—which meant "beautiful land" in French—had withstood the test of time, including the Civil War, hurricanes, river floods, fires, yellow fever and everything else that fell under the heading of "acts of God."

But through it all, God had been good to *Belle Terre.*

Thirty rooms and ten thousand square feet, two-storied and starkly white, with squared, tall cypress columns that measured at least two feet around, and elegant outside central stairways leading up to the second floor, both front and back, it was more than just a house. This place was the local legend and about the only attraction in a village that was fast becoming a ghost town.

Elise didn't see this old mansion as an attraction, even when it was all dressed and shining for the holidays. She only saw it as the house where her father and his four brothers had been born and raised, as the place where her dear grandparents had always lived. Elise remembered long summers of romping up and down these stairs, long summers of lounging in the rickety old swing out underneath the great live oaks that sat like giant green mushrooms throughout the back gardens. She remembered having two coming-out parties. One in Shreveport for the Plantation Ball, and one down here at *Belle Terre,* put on for her especially by *Grand-mère* Melancon so that she could show off her only granddaughter to all her society friends from New Orleans and Baton Rouge.

Elise remembered flowing white dresses on creamy-skinned debutantes, and lemon-scented magnolias floating in crystal bowls filled with water. She remembered giggling girls putting on their makeup in front of a one-hundred-year-old standing oval mirror in one of the many upstairs bedrooms. She remembered tiptoeing down the curving oak stairs late at night, her pink cotton night-gown and robe flying out around her bare feet as she slipped out into the honeysuckle and wisteria-drenched gardens, just so she could stare up at a full Louisiana summer moon.

And she remembered how very much she loved and respected her grandmother, Betty Jean Melancon.

"And that is why I'm here now, *Grand-mère,*" Elise said out loud, her hushed words echoing out into the spacious family room at the center of the mansion. "Because of you."

"I appreciate that," her grandmother said from the hallway, causing Elise to whirl around.

"*Mamere,* I didn't hear you there."

"I've learned how to sneak around my own house, I can assure you," Betty Jean said, the twinkle in her green eyes belying the stern words. "Now what are you mumbling about, child?"

Elise knew the best way to win over her keen grandmother was to be honest. "I want to know why you insisted I come here for Christmas."

"I wanted everyone here with me this year," her grandmother replied, her smile proper and practiced, her back straight as she stood with hands folded together over her gray St. John suit. "It's been much too long since we've had Christmas at *Belle Terre.*"

"But why?" Elise moved around, her designer heels clicking on the aged hardwood floor near the tall windows. "I mean, we've been meeting at Mom and Dad's in Shreveport for Christmas for the last…well, for a very long time now."

They'd done it this way to take some of the burden off her grandmother, to help out with all the preparations in the four years since her grandfather had died. Maybe they'd made a mistake, assuming *Grand-mère* wasn't capable anymore. After all, Elise's parents had insisted they take over the duties once they'd opened the Shreveport office of Melancon Oil and bought their own spacious home in the historical Highland district of Shreveport. Her mother loved showing off and entertaining. And since the rest of the Melancon clan was scattered to the four winds, it had been hard to get them all together over the last few years anyway.

"It has been a long time since we've all gathered here," Elise said, her brow lifting as she lowered her head to stare over at her grandmother.

"Too long," Betty Jean said again, fingering the puffs of white-blonde hair atop her head, her eyes softening with memories. "I wanted everyone here and that's final."

Elise turned to stare at her grandmother. "You look frail. Are you ill? Is that why you summoned me here?"

"Goodness," her grandmother huffed, "I am *old,* Boo. Old and tired. But I can assure you I'm fit as a fiddle."

Elise smiled at being called "Boo." It was a Cajun pet name for "darling" that her grandmother had always reserved just for her. Rushing across the Aubusson rug, Elise hugged her grandmother close.

"I won't live much longer if you cut my breath off," Betty Jean said in a gentle, chuckling protest. "And I will tell you exactly why you're here, if you'll just sit down with me and have a nice cup of tea."

Elise backed away, still wary. "You never drink tea unless there is something on your mind."

"I have something on my mind," Betty Jean said, urging her toward a damask, high-backed peach-colored sofa, her lips tightening into a prim, no-nonsense line. "And I want you to listen good to me before you say no."

Elise knew that look. *Grand-mère* could be intimidating, if one didn't know how to handle her. The woman had served as a state Senator up in Baton Rouge for two terms, and that while raising five boys, some of whom had grown up to work in public service and politics themselves. Those boys had brought her fifteen grandchildren, all male except for Elise. *Grand-mère* could hunt, shoot and fish with the best of them, too. But she could also have a good time at any old *fais do-do,* whenever such a party was thrown together, which was often here in Cajun country. And she could out-pray anyone who attended the stone and cypress Bayou Branche cathedral down the road, her faith as strong and sheltering as the live oaks that graced the drive up to her home.

Betty Jean Melancon was the only woman Elise had ever known who could walk in one door wearing wading boots, khakis and a flannel shirt, and come out another door wearing pearls, a tailored wool sheath and black patent pumps, and look beautiful doing either. The thought of never seeing that face again frightened Elise.

"You're dying. That's it, isn't it?" Elise asked now, already a great void in her heart at the thought.

"I told you, I'm fine," her grandmother reminded her as she poured tea out of the highly polished silver service that had survived the Civil War hidden from the

Yankees in the rich loam near the back bayou. "This has nothing to do with dying, my dear. But…it has everything to do with living."

"*Grand-mère,* you're scaring me," Elise replied, taking her tea in the delicate yellow-rose Royal Kent cup her grandmother handed her.

"Have a sugar cookie, Boo," her grandmother said in response. "And listen while you chew. I only have a few minutes before your parents arrive, and you know how your mother is—all loudness and flash. We need this quiet time before my son brings that woman into my peaceful home."

"Is this about mother then?" Elise asked, wondering what her mother Cissie and her grandmother Betty Jean could possibly be fighting about this time.

"No, not about her," Betty Jean said, shaking her head in that ladylike way that told people to sit up and take notice. "It's more about you."

"Me? What have I done?"

"You haven't done anything yet," her grandmother responded before taking a sip of her cream-laced tea. "It's what I need you to do in the short time you're here."

"Oh, and what is that?" Elise asked, her curiosity piqued.

"I have a project for you, Boo. I've thought about this and decided you are the right person for this job."

"*Grand-mère,* what on earth are you talking about?" Elise asked, her cookie still balanced on the saucer of her teacup.

"Put that down and come to the side window with me,"

Betty Jean said, her glance holding a covert kind of amusement. "I want you to see something."

Elise did as her grandmother asked, wondering if the old dear wanted her to take up gardening.

But what Elise saw there near the Cherokee roses moving up the latticework of the century-old gazebo caused her to gasp. "Who is that?"

"That," her grandmother said with another chuckle, "is the project I want you to take on."

Elise looked at the dark-skinned man working in the flower bed. He was tall and muscular, his hair the sun-streaked brown color of pecan shells, his clothes the washed gray and black that showed they'd been worn over and over again. Although it was chilly and drab outside, the man wore only a faded black T-shirt and work pants, and a little strip of rawhide in his too-long ponytail. "What…what do you want me to do…with *him?*"

Betty Jean held a hand to Elise's teal cashmere sweater. "I want you to…reform him. In time for Christmas dinner here at *Belle Terre.* That gives you less than two weeks. I'd say you'd better get cracking."

# CHAPTER TWO

Theo Galliano felt the hair on the back of his neck standing straight up. Somebody was watching him. He could feel it in his bones. Dropping the rake he'd been using to remove winter-dry leaves from underneath the rose arbor, Theo turned around and looked straight into the tall windows lined up across the downstairs rooms of *Belle Terre*.

And was met with two sets of curious eyes staring back out at him.

*Mais?* Theo thought to himself. Well, Tee, what have you gone and done now, for the great *Mamere* herself to be staring at you with such determination?

And who, he wondered with a kind of delicious thread of warning moving down his spine, was that adorable young lady standing there all debutante proper beside Mrs. M? She had hair the color of rich harvest straw and big blue-green eyes that reminded Theo of the deepest waters of the Gulf.

But why was this beautiful creature staring at him as if he'd turned into a *cochon* with two heads?

Scratching his chin, Theo decided, with what his *maman* would say *was* the stubbornness of a two-headed pig, to meet this challenge head-on. He gave the two lovely women watching him a dashing smile and then he bowed deeply and with a bit of elaborate flourish. Lifting his head, he was rewarded with a return smile and a brisk wave from dear old Mrs. M, while her young friend only glared at him even harder, her eyes going wide with shock and confusion, her pretty mouth moving into an O-shaped kind of surprise.

Gesturing with a dirt-stained hand, Theo mouthed to Mrs. M, then pointed a finger to his chest, tapping it three times. "Do you need me?"

Mrs. M actually giggled in response and nodded. "Yes."

Theo wiped his dirty hands on his equally dirty pants and started strolling toward the back porch, watching out of the corner of his eye as Mrs. M marched her young friend toward the French doors of the kitchen.

"Dis should be interesting," Theo said under his breath. "Very interesting."

"I won't go out there, *Mamere*," Elise said, tugging with both hands to get away from her grandmother's surprisingly strong pull.

"Yes, you will," Betty Jean responded, drenching her with that all-knowing, grandmotherly look. "You will mind your manners and you will behave in the way your mama taught you. At least, I hope that air-brained flutter-ball taught you some manners."

"*Mamere!*" Elise exclaimed, disapproval echoing in the one word. "Why do you insist on calling my mother such horrid names."

"If the shoe fits—" Betty Jean responded, still tugging.

"Oh, you are impossible," Elise said on a hiss of air. "I am not going out there to socialize with that…that swamp rat!"

Betty Jean turned so fast, Elise heard the screeching of her black kidskin pumps hitting the hardwood floors of the kitchen. "Speaking of calling names! Listen to me, Boo. I don't ask much of my family, and I have rarely asked you for such a favor. But you are the only person in the world I can trust to help this poor man out. Now, bear with me while I introduce you." She smiled sweetly, but Elise saw the threat of a tirade underneath that gentle smile. "If you will just think about how important this is to Tee-do—"

"Tee-do? Tee-do?" Elise asked, horrified all over again. "What kind of name is that for a grown man?"

Betty Jean lifted her head to make sure the man hadn't made it to the porch yet. "His *maman* gave him that nickname when he was just a baby. She called him her sweet little one. I can't help it if it stuck." Then she shrugged with an eloquence reserved for soirees and lunches at the club. "Anyway, his real name is Theo, short for Theodore, but we call him Tee now."

"Oh well, I feel ever so much better about things, then," Elise said, still bracing herself for this introduction.

Her grandmother had obviously suffered some sort of affliction—maybe a ministroke or a definite lack of short-term memory. Why else would she insist that Elise not only meet this brut, but also—what was the word *Grand-mère* had used—*reform* him?

"You will feel good about everything if you do this for me," Betty Jean replied, pulling open the back door even as she said the words. "The Lord loves a cheerful giver. Tee is so very adorable, but he needs a little help in the social graces department."

"Let him order a book off eBay, then," Elise replied, dreading this with all her being, and maybe because of the way the man had looked at her...well, it made her feel all funny inside. As if a flock of geese had been set loose in her stomach.

"I can't give him a book, darling," her grandmother said in a low whisper. "I'm not even sure he can actually read. Well, I mean, I know he can read. We often discuss our favorite Bible passages. He has had a bit of formal education. I'm just not sure if he likes to read. Maybe you can encourage him in that area, too."

"Oh, this is just lovely," Elise said, wishing she'd just stayed in North Louisiana. "Why do *I* have to reform him anyway? What's the big occasion?"

Her grandmother turned, pressed a finger to her lips. "His intended is coming home for Christmas and, well, things have been a bit strained since she went off to LSU. Maggie has apparently gotten too big for her britches, so to speak. We have to show her that Tee out there is a good and decent man, the same man she left back in the fall."

It took Elise a minute to decipher her grandmother's old-fashioned terms of explanation. "You mean, I have to get him ready for his girlfriend?"

"Exactly," Betty Jean said, her smile beaming as she turned to greet the man coming up the back steps.

"Well, isn't that just so special," Elise said, her voice exaggerated and exasperated. "I get to train him, then turn him over to another woman."

Betty Jean nodded, still smiling. "I said you were perfect for the job, didn't I, suga'? Mercy, but you've sent some of the best packing without a backward glance. Knowing how prickly you are about men, I knew there'd be no chance of you and Tee falling for each other."

"Perfect," Elise said, her gaze sweeping over the blob of testosterone now standing with a goofy grin on the back porch. "Just perfect."

She was just about as perfect as a woman could get, Theo decided as he did a lazy assessment of the woman standing with Mrs. Melancon. He liked the creamy tan of her fair skin, liked the way her hair ribboned in blonde folds down to her shoulders, liked the way the blue-green of her expensive sweater matched both her eyes and her shoes. In fact, he liked just about everything about this woman.

Then he did a double take. "You remind me of someone."

The woman stared down at him with flared nostrils, as if he were a very ugly stinkbug.

"She does remind you of someone?" Mrs. M asked, her

smile putting out a thousand-watt brilliance. "Think real hard, Tee, and you'll realize who this is."

Tee thought real hard, glanced back up at them, did some comparisons, then let out a whoop and slapped a hand on his dusty pants. "*Mais, jamais d'la vie!* Never in my life would I have guessed, but yes, I see it right there in that pretty smile—and those eyes, *oui*. This is your granddaughter, isn't it, Mrs. M?"

"It is, indeed," Mrs. Melancon said, bobbing her head, even as she sent a definite poke to the dainty ribs of the shell-shocked woman standing with her. "This is our dear Elise Rachelle Melancon, Tee. She's come home for Christmas."

Elise mouthed an "ouch" then rubbed her now-bruised ribs. "*Mamere,* I'm perfectly capable of introducing myself." Then she extended a well-manicured hand to Theo. "I'm Elise Melancon. It's very nice to meet you, Mr. Tee-do."

Theo took her hand, careful not to dirty it up. "It's just Tee now, Miss Elise. I used to be real little and real sweet, but now I'm just real sweet." He followed that proud proclamation with a wide smile and a wink.

Mrs. Melancon let out a hoot of laughter, then glanced with a nervous twitch of her smile toward her granddaughter. "He's a real charmer, our Theo is."

"What should I call you?" Elise asked, yanking her hand back. "What would you prefer, Theo or Tee?"

Theo couldn't tell her what he'd prefer right now, because her *grand-mère* would box his ears at such thoughts. "I'm Theo Galliano," he said, smiling up at them. "But you can call me Tee. I don't mind one bit."

"Call me Elise, then," she replied, her nose so high in the air, Theo figured she'd catch a whiff of his *maman's* gumbo clear over across the bayou.

"Okay, then. Well, it was very nice to meet you, Elise. You know, what with all those boys running around here when Mrs. M's sons come to visit, you hold a special place in her heart, you being the only girl and all."

Theo watched as the woman's haughty expression changed to one of unwavering love for her grandmother. Watched and appreciated that sentiment. He loved her grandmother, too.

"Thank you, Tee," Elise said, a smile finally cracking the frozen expression on her face. "It's good to be home with *Mamere,* I have to admit. I mean, in spite of this hare-brained idea she has to—"

"Oh my, look at the time," Betty Jean said, urging her pretty granddaughter around. "Your parents are due any minute now and I don't have brunch ready."

"But—" Elise said, clearly confused. "I thought—"

"You thought about the crescent rolls. I reckon they're ready for the oven."

Theo saw the warning look Mrs. Melancon gave Elise. "Is everything all right?" he asked. "Did you need me for something, Mrs. M?"

"Oh, no. Just wanted you to meet Elise. I hope you two can become better acquainted, say later today. Why don't you come for supper tonight, Tee? Just a pot of shrimp Creole and some good homemade multigrain bread, and maybe apple pie for dessert?"

Theo had to shake his head. He'd had his share of

meals with Mrs. Melancon, but never when family was home. "You want me to come to supper, tonight?"

"Yes. Is seven okay for you?"

Theo looked at Elise, then turned back to her grandmother. "Mrs. M, are you trying to set me up with your lovely granddaughter here?"

Mrs. Melancon feigned surprise, but Theo saw the sparkle in her eyes. He also saw the soft blush moving down Elise Melancon's neck.

"Heavens no, Theo. I just thought that…well…since you have company coming to town for the holidays, and since you told me last week that you might could use some help in the…social graces department, and well, since Elise has been to finishing school, not to mention being taught everything I know about etiquette, well, that she might give you a few pointers. That's all."

Theo felt the implications of that sidestepping explanation all the way down to his work boots. Then understanding dawned on him. "You mean, this is the 'coach' you told me you'd hire to help me learn manners? Is this the one, Mrs. M?"

Mrs. Melancon looked flustered for about two seconds, then lifted her head to a regal angle. "Yes, Theo, as a matter of fact, this is the very one. Elise had agreed to help teach you everything you need to know in order to show off for your Maggie. I hope you won't be offended by this offer."

Theo shook his head again. He didn't know whether to be offended or tickled silly. And he didn't know how to tell dear Mrs. M that he and Maggie had broken up just last night, after he'd learned over the phone, no less, and in no uncertain terms, that she needed some time and space away from Theo.

Theo looked from Mrs. Melancon's hopeful face to Elise Melancon's doubtful one. He liked a good challenge. And he really, really liked Elise Melancon. What could it hurt if he went along with this unselfish gesture of kindness and let her show him the ways of her world—for just a little while?

And what could it hurt if he did learn a few manners to show snobby Maggie Aguillard he could change? No, Theo thought with a bit of mischief, it couldn't hurt at all to have a little etiquette class with cute Elise Melancon.

She could show him manners and he…well, he could show her all about real life. And show Maggie a thing or two.

So he looked at Mrs. Melancon and shrugged.

"Maggie and I broke up. But maybe if I become a bit more refined, I can win her back, *oui?*"

*"Oui,"* Mrs. Melancon replied, her head bobbing.

"Oh, all right," Elise replied, her gaze sympathetic in spite of her tone.

What a joyous Christmas this was going to be.

# CHAPTER THREE

"**W**hy is the yardman coming for dinner?" Cissie Melancon asked as she looked through the slice of air at the swinging doors from the kitchen to the dining room. "Doesn't he usually just help *serve* dinner? *Mamere,* have you lost some of your faculties?"

"I've got more brain cells than you do natural blond hairs, I can assure you," Betty Jean said, her voice steely, her smile pleasant as she buttered dinner rolls with a flourish.

"Very funny," Cissie replied, bringing a protective hand to her honey-gold glitzed bob. "I was born a natural blonde, you know."

"And I was born with good sense in my head," Betty Jean countered, her smile still intact.

"Now, Mama," her son, Quincy, said from his perch on a kitchen stool, "are you and Cissie going to exchange insults the whole time we're here, or are you going to behave?"

His mother looked petulant for a second, then beamed a mother's smile at her fifth son. "*I* plan on behaving. You'll have to remind your lovely wife to do the same. And that means she will be kind and polite to anyone I happen to invite for dinner."

Cissie rolled her heavily shadowed eyes. "Well, I declare, I just don't see how the gardener can make for a good dinner companion. I mean, that man is about half-wild, from the looks of him."

Elise listened to this exchange with a growing feeling of anxiety. What would her prim and proper mother think when *Grand-mère* announced her loopy plan for Elise to re-form the half-wild yardman who'd just entered the dining room and was even now making jokes with Reginald, the butler?

"Shouldn't one of us go and greet the poor man?" Quincy asked, still reading over the paper.

Since her father didn't act as if he should be the one to do so, Elise threw up her hands. "Goodness, I'll go and talk to our guest. If *Grand-mère* wants him here, then we'd better entertain him until dinner is ready."

Her grandmother inclined her head. "How very thought-ful *you* are, dear. Thank you." She gave her daughter-in-law and her son a disapproving look. "He doesn't bite, you know."

"Are you sure about that?" Cissie asked from her vantage point near the doors. "He's so big and wiry, all muscle and lean like that. What does one feed such a man?"

Quincy laughed, then threw the paper down. "Anything he asks for, I imagine."

In spite of her own concerns and doubts regarding the Cajun, Elise felt she had to come to his defense. Her snobbish parents could be so cruel at times. "Theo Galliano is a very interesting man, Mama. *Grand-mère* tells me he went away to school for a while, but he had to come home recently to help support the family. It seems they struggle, what with being shrimpers and fishermen."

"That's a tough life," her father said, nodding in that way that told her he was extremely glad he didn't have to live that way.

And neither did she, thanks to the Melancon oil and gas lines scattered throughout these swamps and bayous. Wondering why that should make her feel guilty instead of glad, Elise whirled past her snooping mother. "Excuse me."

Cissie eyed her daughter with horror. "Surely you're not really going in there?"

"Of course I am," Elise said, giving her mother a smug look. "I do have manners, after all."

"Precisely," her grandmother said on a chortle of laughter. "I knew you'd understand."

"Understand what?" Cissie said, her nose going up as if she smelled something fishy. "What have you two cooked up?"

"Nothing for you to worry your pretty head about," Betty Jean replied, her gaze centered on the marinated green beans she was preparing for dinner. "Oh, and Elise, tell Reginald to hurry back in here. I think the rice for the Creole is just about ready."

Elise nodded, then pushed at the door, thinking that

message would serve as a perfect excuse for showing up in the dining room. Not that she needed an excuse, of course, to walk into her grandmother's stately dining room.

At the swish of the door, both old Reginald with his laughing gray eyes and Tee or Theo, or whoever he was with his flashing black eyes, turned to stare.

"Now there's a pretty picture, young man," Reginald said, his deep southern drawl lifting up to the tall ceilings. "A true southern belle."

"*Oui,*" Theo replied, his gaze sweeping over Elise's navy blue flared dinner dress with apparent appreciation.

Enough appreciation to make her blush and finger her pearls.

"Hello, Theo," she said, making an instant decision to call him by his given name, which she had no doubt was only part of his real name. "We didn't realize you had arrived."

"I've been having a bit of fun with Reggie here," Theo said, his eyes twinkling.

*Reggie.* He was calling suave, stuffy Reginald Armand, a man who'd been trained in England, a man who came from a long line of dignified, distinguished butlers with stiff upper lips and pedigrees that dated back to kings and queens—he was calling him *Reggie.*

Elise looked from Theo's mirthful face to Reginald's serene one. No looking down his nose here. No swift, sharp reprimands, either. The butler, who was certainly lovable and endearing, if not somewhat disapproving at times, was chuckling. Chuckling!

"Well, what were you two talking about?"

Reginald stood up straight, then cleared his throat. "A bit of off-color humor, I'm afraid, Miss Elise. Beg your pardon."

"Don't apologize, please," Elise replied, still amazed that Theo could cause the oh-so-proper butler to actually laugh. "But you could clue me in on the joke."

"Oh, naw, naw," Theo said, raising a hand, his laughter causing his broad chest to shake. "It's not proper to share this particular redneck joke with a lady."

"No, indeed," Reginald said, looking chagrined. "I'd better get back into the kitchen."

Elise nodded. "Yes, *Grand-mère* was asking for you. Something about the rice?"

"Oh, dear," Reginald said, bringing his hands to his face. "I do hope I haven't scorched it. I do so hate sticky rice."

Elise felt as if she'd been scorched, and she knew things in here were much more sticky than the rice, by the way Theo Galliano was looking at her. "Would you like to join my family—in the kitchen?"

"The kitchen?" He shrugged. "Now I would have thought they'd be having high tea in the front parlor."

"We're not so formal as that," Elise replied, feeling the sting of his implied words. "We're very relaxed here at *Belle Terre*." She did try to relax, just to prove her point.

"Is that why you haven't been around in a blue moon?"

She whirled at the door, only to find him two steps behind her. Too close. And much too personal. "What are you implying?" she asked, noting the clean, soapy smell surrounding him. He'd cleaned up. White button-up shirt, pressed jeans.

"Me, nothing." He shrugged. "It's just that I respect Mrs. M. And it's just that's she's been mighty lonely since Mr. M passed on, is all."

"We're well aware of that," Elise said, her neck stiffening with guilt and awareness. "And that's one of the reasons we all agreed to have Christmas here."

"*Ça c'est bon,*" he said, his eyes telling her that it was her business, after all. "Good to hear. Me, I can't imagine spending the blessed Noel anywhere but right here on the bayou."

Still stinging, Elise said, "Well, perhaps that's why *Mamere* wants me to help you. Perhaps you might impress your girlfriend if you tried leaving the bayou once and a while."

He gave her a look that made her want to run away, the black of his eyes piercing her with scorn. "Perhaps," he said. Then he opened the door for her. "Maybe we'd better get into the kitchen with the others."

Elise wished she hadn't made that remark. It was very pointed, but it was the truth. The man obviously hadn't been up past Breaux Bridge, or he'd know that there were many ways to communicate with family, even if one didn't get to come home as often. Why, there was e-mail and telephones and even cards and letters. Elise had called her grandmother on a weekly basis and sent her nice cards and gifts on special occasions.

But you weren't here, that small voice inside her head said, causing her to glare over at the man escorting her into the massive, too-warm kitchen.

And he was, that same voice replied. He was here with

your grandmother, laughing with her and spending time with her, while all of her own children and grandchildren were too busy to do so. That made Elise very jealous and resentful, for some strange reason. Well, *she* was certainly here now. And she'd do whatever her grandmother asked, if it would make Betty Jean happy.

Even resort to "training" this man in the ways of the world. *I'll try, Lord. But I'll need Your help.*

But as she glanced over at Theo and saw the way his black eyes danced over her face with both anticipation and condemnation, Elise wondered what exactly she was supposed to teach Theo Galliano.

And she wondered just what the man could show her, in the ways of the bayou.

He'd show her a thing or two, Theo decided as they sat down to the casual dinner. Cissie Melancon glared at him while her husband, the dashing Quincy, talked to the open air about the stock market and the continuing oil crisis in the Middle East. Mrs. M smiled and remained as gracious as ever. And Elise, well, she just sat there staring down at her food as if it held something very distasteful in it.

"Dis is good," Theo said, then covered his mouth.

"Did you just belch?" Cissie asked, that look of horror on her face pinning Theo to his chair.

"*Non,* I managed to keep that one down," he replied with a grin. "But my *maman* says it's sure a compliment to the cook if the food causes—"

"More bread?" Elise said, grabbing at the breadbasket so fast she almost knocked over her water glass.

"*Non,* I'm good," Theo replied, making sure he gave her a long, thorough look just so he could watch her blush underneath the chandeliers.

Her mother let an obvious but very delicate shudder erupt from her scrawny shoulders. "Where are your people from, Mr. Galliano?"

"Right here. Bayou Branche has always been our home," he replied. "We live in a little house not much bigger than this room and your kitchen there, I imagine. It's up on stilts, since the wetlands keep creeping right into our door."

Cissie Melancon obviously didn't know how to respond to that. She took a long drink of her iced tea and busied herself with buttering another roll.

Quincy Melancon gave Theo a hard, calculating look, but remained silent.

"We're so glad you joined us," Betty Jean said for about the tenth time. "I just love having this house full of visitors."

Theo nodded, took his bread and dipped it all around his nearly empty bowl of gumbo, sopping up the rich brown roux as he grinned over at Cissie. "For true, this is almost as good as my own *maman's.*"

He'd planned on embarrassing all of them as he slurped up the gravy and bread. He'd planned wrong.

Elise Melancon and her grandmother, as if in unison, both proceeded to do the same thing with their bread and roux. As Elise bit into her gravy-sodden bread, she let out a soft moan. "Mmm, this is very good. And now I've learned a new way to get to the bottom of that rich roux."

"Elise," her mother said, dropping her hands on the table, "I know I raised you better than that." Then mortified, she glanced over at Theo, then clamped her mouth shut.

Apple pie was next. Theo planned on eating his without the help of a spoon or fork. He'd just pick the whole piece up and shove it into his mouth the way he always did whenever his *maman* pulled a fresh pie from the oven. He'd love to see the lovely Elise do that. He'd show her that he really needed that manners course. And that way, she'd have to agree to spend more time with him. Just to train him.

# CHAPTER FOUR

"Just how do you expect me to do this, *Mämere?*" Elise asked the next morning after breakfast. "Mother will suspect something right off if she sees me spending time with the Cajun."

Thinking back over their awkward dinner last night, Elise wondered if her mother didn't already suspect something. Cissie had kept a slanted eye on both her daughter and their mysterious guest.

"And besides," Elise continued, "the Cajun seems to have adequate manners, even if he did practically drink his soup from his bowl last night. At least he managed to make polite conversation, just with a heavy dialect."

In fact, Theo Galliano had seemed right at home eating the hearty meal served on the everyday casual china. He had slurped, of course, and he had almost belched just that once, but he hadn't talked with his mouth full. Okay, except for that whole slice of pie he'd managed to eat without the benefit of a fork, in between thanking *Grand-*

*mère* and grinning at Elise's shocked-speechless mother. But he had stared a lot—that was indeed rude. Mostly at Elise.

"His name is Theo, dear," Betty Jean reminded her with a kind glance. "Theodore Emile Galliano, to be exact. He is one of seven children, four boys and three girls. And yes, their Christian parents have taught them manners, but with that many in a small house, one can only do so much."

"Mercy," Elise replied as she finished wrapping one of the many presents her grandmother had out on the kitchen table. "Why have I never met any of these people before?"

Betty Jean laughed and waved a hand. "When you were little and came to visit, it was all I could do to get your mama to let you go outside and play, let alone have you associate with the poor family across the bayou. The Galliano family has lived on this land as long as I can remember, but they always kept to themselves. I'd send them over food and gifts at Christmas, and they'd return the favor by sending one of the boys over with fresh seafood or some boudin—things like that. Other than that, we pretty much left each other alone until recent years."

"What happened to make that change?" Elise asked, curious but cautious.

Her grandmother's eyes seemed to sadden as Betty Jean stared down at the shiny wrapping spread on the table.

"Hard times, that's what happened," Betty Jean explained. "As I told you, Theo had gone off to college, up at Nicholls State in Thibodaux. He'd saved up for years after high school, and took out student loans to pay his way. Plus, he had an anonymous donor to help him some."

She shrugged and smiled, clearly telling Elise *she* was probably that donor. "After your grandfather died, Theo's mother Deidre sent him over with some food. We had a good long talk that night, Theo and I. I realized his faith is very solid and sure. He told me all about wanting to go to college, to better himself, told me that he and Maggie had big plans. After that, he'd come by about once a week to help me with the gardens, do little odd jobs around the house. He was so proud the day he left for college. He made it to his senior year, but then his father, Emile, Sr.—they call him Easy for some reason—well, he got hurt in a boating accident and took months to recover. Even after his recovery, he was still in a lot of pain. That left the family in a bad way, what with the time off work and the hospital bills to pay. The younger brothers and sisters tried to pitch in, but after a few months, it was up to Theo as the oldest to come home and help the family. So he did, without hesitation."

Elise took this information in, thinking that was a big sacrifice for a son. But then, what else could he do? She hadn't hesitated to take a position with the family company, but then that had more or less been handed to her on a silver platter. Theo hadn't had a choice in the matter. "What was Theo studying at school?"

"Marine biology," Betty Jean replied, pride shining in her eyes. "That boy loves the great outdoors. He wants to work to protect his little piece of the world."

Elise was stunned. "I thought you said you weren't sure he could even read."

Betty Jean chuckled. "Oh, that. I was just trying to make you feel sorry for him."

Elise gave her grandmother a reprimanding look, her brow slanting as she shook her finger. "You're telling me that Theo came close to being a marine biologist and he gave it all up to work the shrimp boats?"

"That's pretty much the whole story," her grandmother said, nodding. "He's twenty-eight and still searching for a way to better himself. He told me he aims to go back one day and get that degree. And I believe he will do it."

"With your help," Elise said, coming around the table to hug her grandmother. "You are a very kind neighbor, *Mamere.*"

Betty Jean shrugged again. "What else is an old woman to do? I'm here in this big place, with a lot of time on my hands and a lot of money in my bank account. I would gladly help the Galliano family with their bills, but Emile has too much pride to accept that kind of charity."

Pushing away her own guilt, Elise asked, "So you've made it your mission to help Theo."

"More or less."

"I love you," Elise said, tears springing to her eyes.

"Then do me this one favor," Betty Jean said, patting Elise on the back. "Spend some time with Theo and help him gain his self-confidence back. He's a good man, but he's a bit shy and reserved. And that Maggie—she's a handful, let me tell you. We have to show her a good impression."

"But if she loves him—"

"She loved him when he was planning a future with a

good job. Things have changed now. Theo thinks they're drifting apart. He thinks Maggie is ashamed of him. And now she's gone and broken his heart."

Elise felt her hackles rising. "Well, if she's that shallow, maybe Theo should just forget about her."

"He loves her," Betty Jean said, her eyes taking on a sparkling quality that made Elise suspicious. "But, who knows. As I said, things change."

Elise slapped a hand on the table. "Things are going to change. I'll take on this project, *Mamere*. Consider it my Christmas present to you, to help Theo win back his Maggie."

"I couldn't ask for anything more," Betty Jean replied, her smile beaming as bright as the twinkling lights on the tiny Christmas tree by the window in the kitchen. "He'll be over here this afternoon to finish stringing the lights out front. You might approach him then. Oh, and you might want to keep this just between us, dear." Betty Jean lifted her eyes toward the upstairs. "You know how highstrung your mother can be at times."

"Okay," Elise said, leaning close. "She'll never even notice a thing."

But Elise knew Cissie Melancon. Her mother's fondest hope was to marry her socialite daughter off to a senator or doctor, preferably someone with a lineage that dated back to before the Civil War. Someone with royal connections would be even better. Cissie would never cotton to her daughter spending time with a man who made his living from shrimping and working part-time odd jobs.

"This is going to be a very interesting Christmas," Elise said as she stole a sugar cookie from Reginald's secret stash. "Very interesting."

Theo knew she was watching him. He also knew that she had big plans for him. All he had to do was wait to see what those plans required. Watch and pray, he told himself.

So this pretty little sweetheart was going to teach him all about proper manners. It wasn't like he didn't have manners. He knew which fork went where, even if his *maman* didn't have a matching set of silver utensils. And he knew the important things—to be kind and show respect, to do a good day's honest work, and to be loyal to his family and to trust in God, always.

What else could a man ask for?

But when Theo turned and saw Elise Melancon standing on the long, wide back porch of *Belle Terre,* his gut twisted with such a sweet longing, he knew there was a lot more a man could ask for. A whole lot more.

She was wearing a white sweater trimmed with fluffy pink fur at the collar, and matching white wool pants that probably cost more than a whole month's worth of shrimping could buy. Her kid leather shoes were a soft muted pink, to match her sweater, no doubt, with tiny little heels and pointed toes that made her feet look dainty. All dressed up like a pretty doll. And looking at him with those wide ocean-eyes. Looking at him with questions and doubts, and maybe a little fear and loathing.

Don't be foolish, he told himself as he smiled and tipped

his hand to her. He'd lost Maggie because of bad luck and bad timing. How could he even expect a woman like Elise Melancon to want to associate with the likes of him?

"Don't expect much and that's exactly what you'll get."

His mother's words seemed to echo over the live oaks and cottonwoods. He could almost feel her boxing his ears in that affectionate but firm way Deidre had.

Sure, Theo thought, his remorse and resentment bubbling up like swamp mire. He'd had big expectations, and he'd still lost out on his hopes and dreams. He'd lost Maggie. It was enough to make a man bitter for life.

It was enough to make a man lash out.

And so he did. At the woman standing there watching him. The same woman who'd sat watching him from across the dinner table last night, her quick glances coy and cryptic, her quick wit charming and above reproach. Or more like, *unapproachable.*

Theo was determined to break through that cool resolve.

"What's the matter, lady? Never seen a man trying to untangle Christmas lights before?"

She blushed as she started down the steps toward him.

"I'm so sorry. I...I didn't mean to stare. It's just that well—"

Theo threw down the white lights he'd been coaxing around a huge tree trunk. "It's just that you really don't want to do as your *grand-mère* asked. It's just that you really don't want to be seen with the likes of *moi,* right? It's just that you'd rather walk right into quicksand then spend one minute trying to tame me, right?"

She looked surprised, affronted and, finally, angry. Theo watched as the play of emotions moved over her perfect oval face like a sunset washing over the horizon, all shades of blush and cream, all bright and glistening with shimmering clarity. "Yes, I guess it is all of that," she said, throwing him off balance with her honesty.

Theo laughed out loud, which seemed to make her even more mad. "You don't have to do this, you know."

"Yes, I do," she said, coming inches closer. "I promised *Mamere*—"

"I seen promises broken," he said, wishing he hadn't.

"I don't break my promises," she responded, her tone superior and condescending. "It's just that, well, I'm not sure where to start."

Theo stalked the two feet between them, then leaned down close. "Why not start at the beginning. For example, what would a gentleman do in a situation such as this one?"

He could tell by the way her long lashes fluttered that she wasn't exactly sure what a *lady* should do in this situation, let along a gentleman. After all, he was too close. He could smell the sweet floral scent of her expensive perfume. It made him think of a garden full of honeysuckle and lilies.

She swayed, ran a hand over her curling hair. "What do you mean?"

"I mean," he said, inching even closer, a hint of what his *maman* would call *canille*—mischief—making him more daring, "what would a gentleman do if he wanted to kiss a lady, but he didn't know that lady well enough to kiss her?"

She backed away, brushing her hands down the front of her sweater as if to rid them of something disgusting. "A gentleman would never be that stupid in the first place," she said, the breathless quality of her words rushing over him like a soothing wind. "Especially when he's trying to win back another woman."

"Well, then, there you have it," he said with a flourish of his hand in the air. "I guess that proves I ain't a gentleman, after all. And I guess that means that I need your help, Miss Elise. *Bad.*"

That word seemed to lift out over the trees in a warning echo as Theo watched her turn and rush into the house with a slamming of the door. He'd lashed out. And she'd shut him out, that was for sure.

# CHAPTER FIVE

~∞◎∞~

She was back in five minutes.

Theo went on with his business. He had to get these lights up before the rest of the Melancon clan came for the Christmas celebration. They'd be dropping in and out, coming and going. They all had busy, glamorous lives and very little time to sit still and enjoy the blessings of the holidays. It was Theo's job to make sure the whole house looked festive and polished for the various gatherings. He had lots to keep him busy. Lots.

She was staring at him again.

He could feel her eyes on him. It reminded him of the time he was walking alone on the sandy lane leading from *Belle Terre* to his house and he'd felt something watching him. That something had turned out to be a sleek Florida panther, a rare sight in the swamps these days.

Theo now felt as if he'd stumbled on something else that was very rare. The perfect woman. All prepped and trained to be almost robotic in her etiquette and her social standing. There had to be a way to break through all that cool layering to get to the heart of the woman. He'd gotten her flustered during this first round.

Time for round two.

He whirled and caught her red-handed. She flinched and looked away.

"Back for more, *chère?*" he asked in such a sweet way, the cool December air seemed to still. "You know, a lady wouldn't stare that way."

"I...I won't be swayed or intimidated," she said, coming down the steps again, her head lifted in an uppity manner that only added to her cuteness. "We need to discuss some things. For example, you need a haircut. I've scheduled you an appointment in the village, with Ginger at Ginger's Bayou Beauties. You know the place, I'm sure."

He shook his head. Women always wanted to change a man right off. "I'm not going to that beauty shop. My brothers would laugh me outta the parish. Besides, my *maman* trims my hair now and again."

"You are going. If you want to impress your Maggie, then you can't look like a caveman. No disrespect to your mother, of course, but a gentleman always has a neat, trimmed haircut."

He turned his head sideways at her. "I told you I wasn't a gentleman."

"And I promised my grandmother I'd help you become one."

Silent and scowling, he went back to trying to twist lights around the nearest tree trunk, throwing in a couple of he-man grunts for good measure.

"After the haircut, we'll go shopping. We'll have to drive into New Orleans." She studied one of her French-manicured nails. "The Dollar Hollow in the village simply won't do."

"I buy my jeans there," he pointed out, the batch of lights he'd just unstrung seeming to tangle in his white-fisted grip. "My shirts and shoes, too."

"You can't wear those horrid faded jeans to a formal Christmas dinner."

Frustrated at her high-handed, snobbish attitude, Theo threw down the strand of lights. "*Non*, but I don't need some fancy outfit that costs an arm and a leg. I have some nice dress shirts that I wear to church. Why won't one of dem do?"

She slanted her aquamarine eyes down on him. "Because dem—them—those—aren't the right kind of shirts for a gentleman. You need something tailored and fitted to—" her gaze skimmed over his chest "—to your shoulders and arms."

"I always just eyeball the size," he said with a shrug. This "gentleman" business was way too complicated.

"That's the problem, Theo," she said as she pranced toward him. "You can't eyeball good taste."

"Well, then mebbe I don't need to get good taste," he responded, wondering how the tables had been turned so he was now the one on the defensive.

"We'll have to work on your diction, too," she said, her eyes gleaming with victory. "You need to learn to articulate your words, not slur them together in a mumbo jumbo of cluttered Cajun-French and broken English."

*"Oo ye yi,"* Theo said, stringing lights with all his might, stringing them so tight the poor tree would probably have permanent marks. "I'm so sorry that you can't comprehend what I'm saying to you, suga'." He wanted to say a few more things, things she'd understand in no uncertain terms, but then, he reminded himself that this stuck-up beauty was Betty Jean's granddaughter. Out of respect for her *mamere,* he kept those thoughts to himself. In a slow, deliberately drawn out drawl, he added, "What exactly is it that you don't understand about me, Miss Elise?"

"Everything," she said with a huffy shrug, a becoming flush of pink rising up her face. "I mean, you had so much going for you, Theo, from what *Mamere* has told me. You went to college. I know you must be smart. Why do you act so, so—"

*"Stupide?"* He threw down the rest of the lights, then turned to glare at her, the pressure building inside his chest causing him to take a deep breath. "That's what you think, *oui?* You feel sorry for poor Theo, the Cajun boy who had to give up his dreams to come home and help the family? Is that how you see me, as someone who just gave up? Someone too dumb to see what he had in front of his face?"

Anger made him stomp close, his finger in her face. "Let me tell you something, right here, right now. You do not need to feel sorry for me. I am a happy man. A very happy man. I love my family. I will do whatever it takes to see them through this rough spot. That's what family is all about. But then, I reckon you've never had to deal with such things, have you, princess?" Seeing the mist of embarrassment in her eyes, he leaned even closer. "Did you understand that? Did I say it in the right way? Do you think you could wipe that look of pity off your face and understand that I don't need the likes of you doing me any favors?"

"I'm doing this for my grandmother," Elise replied, her eyelashes fluttering as she batted back what looked like anger. "I'm doing this as *a favor to her.*"

"*Oui,* that's very kind of you. But, me, I'm thinking the deal is off. I'm thinking mebbe I don't need any manners training from someone like you."

Her eyes widened. "What do you mean, someone like me?"

He pushed and pushed until he had her up against a square column. "I mean, *chère,* that I like my women down-to-earth and honest. I like them sweet and pleasant. I like to laugh with a woman, and share my heart with her. I like to be on the same level, two hearts, one purpose. I can't see that happening with you, even though you are mighty tempting and as pretty as a morning glory. I can't—"

"No one ever implied we'd…that we'd become…that you and I…we're just…I'm not interested in—"

"Oh, right," he said, laughing as he kept her pinned to the post. "You're just here to make sure I behave and change my bad ways, *oui?* You feel an obligation to help me, because your dear *grand-mère* asked you to do this. And you can't turn her down, maybe because your heart is telling you that you've neglected her and now you feel really bad about all of that? Is that the way of it, *catin?*"

She gave him a direct look that caused her blue-green eyes to blaze like a fire's tip. "You think you know me so well, don't you, Theo? You think I'm just a shallow socialite who's never had to work for anything, right?"

"*Oui*, that's about right."

She looked away. "You don't know me at all, then." But when she looked back at him, he thought he saw defeat there in her eyes. "I'm blessed to be born into a wealthy family, no doubt. But I've worked hard for my family, too. Not in the same way as you, but hard nevertheless, because I love them. Maybe you can't understand me, but don't you think you're the one who's a snob, judging me just because our lives are so different?"

Theo backed up, took a breath. She was right. He was judging her. And he'd been really mean to tease her and flirt with her. And deep inside, he couldn't disappoint her grandmother. The woman had been his friend and his mentor for several years. He'd walk through a gator-infested swamp to please Betty Jean Melancon. Besides, it was only two weeks or so. Surely he could handle Elise for that small amount of time.

They stood silent for a few breaths, their eyes locking in an unspoken battle of wills. Theo had to give the blonde credit. She didn't back down easily.

"I'm sorry," he finally said. "I won't act up again. What time is the hair appointment?"

"You'll go?" she asked, surprise coloring her creamy skin a glistening pink.

"I'll go. I could use a good trim. And that Ginger, well, it for sure will be nice to have her hands in my hair."

"Thank you," she said, the lifting of her elegantly arched brows the only sign that he'd shocked her. She straightened and turned to walk back into the house. "Lunch will be ready in an hour. We'll go into the village after we eat."

"I have my own lunch," he countered. "I'd prefer to take my meals out here, by myself, from now on."

"Oh, okay then. I'll see you this afternoon." She turned at the back door. "And Theo, I don't feel sorry for you, not at all. I…I admire you. Very much."

Theo knew he was in serious trouble. How could a man resist a compliment like that, all wrapped up inside an explanation and a gracious admission, said from a mouth so pretty and pink it made a man think of plums and strawberries? And said by a woman with eyes the shade of pure water and clear blue skies?

How was a man supposed to behave and resist that kind of package?

*Dear Lord, give me strength,* Theo silently prayed. *Help me to keep my mouth shut and my eyes to myself, Lord. That woman is way out of my league. Way out of my reach. I need Your intervention, Jesus.*

"And I need my head examined," he said, yanking another strand of glittering lights.

When he happened to glance up again, he saw Elise standing at the window, looking out at him. Theo looked away. When he turned back, she was gone.

# CHAPTER SIX

"*Grand-mère,* I don't think I can do this."

"Oh, all you have to do it twist the bread into a little bow, darling."

Elise shook her head. "I'm not talking about making dinner rolls. I don't think I can work with Theo."

"Difficult, is he?"

Elise didn't appreciate the gleam of mirth in her grand-mother's eyes. "That's just the beginning. He thinks I feel pity for him. Have you considered that we're insulting him by doing this?"

"It's no insult to offer help to a friend, sweetie."

"But he seems to resent me so much."

"He resents his lot in life," Betty Jean said, her tiny fingers busy making pretty homemade yeast rolls. "How's that crawfish coming, Reginald?"

On the other side of the long kitchen, Reginald was busy putting the finishing touches on his famous seafood stuffing. It would go with the massive turkey Reginald and

Theo would fry up Cajun style on a big cooker out back. "Crawfish and shrimp are in, Mrs. Melancon. Oysters go in next. Then I'll stir up the sausage. This batch should cool nicely and be ready for the freezer this afternoon."

"Smells delicious," Betty Jean said. Then she turned back to Elise. "Just keep at Theo. He'll come around."

Elise looked down at the lopsided bow of dough she'd tried to twist. "But why is this so important to you, *Mamere?* There must be something you're not telling me."

Betty Jean sent a covert glance toward the ever-listening butler on the other side of the room, then turned up the dial on the radio station that continued to blast Christmas hymns out over the big kitchen. "Well, I do have a confession to make," she said, looking contrite. "I have an ulterior motive for asking you to do this."

"I knew it," Elise said, slapping down the blob of dough in front of her. "Tell me everything, before I make a complete idiot of myself with Theo."

Betty Jean continued to twist the bowknots into precise little rolls. "You remember when you were young, dear. You used to tell me that you wanted to live here with me forever."

Wondering what this had to do with Theo, Elise nodded. "I remember. I wanted to stay at *Belle Terre* and run Melancon Oil and Gas right from the back porch."

"Yes, well, that all changed when you went up to college at Centenary. Then your father moved to the Shreveport office, and well, you've all made a good life up in Shreveport."

Elise wiped the flour and dough off her hands, then looked over at her grandmother. "But?"

"But, I've been thinking. It sure would be nice to have a woman in the local office of Melancon Oil and Gas."

Elise blinked, her mouth falling open. "I must have heard that wrong."

"No, no, you heard right," Betty Jean said inside a chuckle. "I mean, I have enough men and boys around to start my own football team, and I intend to let any and all who are willing be a part of the team. But you're so smart, dear, and you've done such a wonderful job up in Shreveport. I was thinking I could make you head of our Environmental and Ecological Department."

Elise blinked again. "*Mamere,* we don't have an environmental and ecological department."

"Oh, but we would, if you'd agree to head it up," Betty Jean pointed out. "These wetlands are in serious danger, darling. Just ask Theo. That's one reason he went to college. He wants to work to save the land he loves. Did I already mention that?"

"You did. But I still don't see what that has to do with me 'reforming' him, or how my working down here could possibly help when we don't even have that department."

"I aim to create the department. I'm going to present it at the next board meeting, which is next month, by the way. And I aim to hire Theo and let him work his way through the rest of his college term. Then I'll promote him once he gets his degree. I still control fifty-one percent of the stock and so I can appoint anyone I see fit to head up a new department. But I wanted him to gain his confidence back and go back to finish school. That's why I need you to help him, dear. He'll listen to you."

*"Grand-mère—"*

"What time is it?" came a feeble wail from the pocket doors leading out into the hallway.

Elise and Betty Jean turned to find Cissie standing there, her white satin sleep mask pushed up on her forehead, her hair all sleep-tousled. She was wearing a bright purple silk robe and feathery house slippers.

"High time for decent folks to be out of bed," Betty Jean said. Then she shot Elise a warning look and put one finger to her mouth to indicate that they didn't need to discuss this any further. "We'll talk more later," she whispered. "Cissie, the coffee's been on for two hours, but help yourself."

Cissie stumbled with a dramatic flair toward the coffeepot, then plopped onto a wrought-iron barstool by the counter. "Reginald, two spoons of sweetener and lots of cream, please."

Reginald rolled his eyes in disapproval, but went to fetch Cissie's coffee. "Would you care for a bran muffin, Miss Cissie?"

"Bran? Heavens, no," Cissie replied, shaking her head. "I'm on that new diet—the one where you give up carbs— and I know for a fact that your bran muffins are full of carbs."

"They're good for your digestive system," Betty Jean said with a prim smile. Then she eyed Cissie's waistline. "You know, they keep you from being so bloated."

Cissie sat up straight. "Am I bloated? Elise, do I look bloated?"

Elise glared at her grandmother. "Mother, you look fine."

"I'll have bacon, crisp, and one half slice of toast, dry," Cissie instructed the hovering Reginald. "And some fresh fruit would be nice—for my bloated state." She lifted her brows toward Betty Jean. "I've been under such stress, you can't imagine."

"No, can't begin to imagine," Betty Jean said as she handed Reginald a baking sheet of rolls. "Why don't you tell us all about it."

"Well," Cissie said, lounging back against her chair, her steaming coffee in one hand, "I was the chairperson of our Christmas cantata this year. I can't tell you what a chore that was—fifty-five choir members, dozens of unruly children running around, and a minister who is constantly worrying about how much money is coming into the church. It's enough to make a sane woman turn stark raving mad."

"Know any sane women?" Betty Jean asked Elise with a wink.

Cissie frowned, but continued her long, drawn-out account of her hectic life—the social whirl of party obligations, the many fund-raisers where she simply must be seen, the many trips to find suitable clothes to wear to all the holiday social events. "I tell you, I'll be glad when Christmas is over."

Betty Jean stood perfectly still. "You shouldn't make such a remark, Cissie."

"Why on earth not?" Cissie said, her hand busy at her sleep mask.

"Because this special season is not about parties and frocks, or seeing and being seen. It's about Jesus Christ. Or have you forgotten?"

Cissie looked sheepish. "*Mamere,* you know I'm a very devout Christian."

"No, I didn't know that for sure," Betty Jean replied. "I'll rest better now that you've told me though."

"I'm sorry," Cissie said, nibbling her toast. "I haven't forgotten. And in case I didn't say it before, I'm so glad we decided to come here to *Belle Terre* for Christmas. It does bring back the true meaning of the season."

Betty Jean seemed content with that declaration. Elise walked over to her mother. "Sometimes we forget what's important, don't we, Mommy?"

Cissie laughed and hugged her daughter. "Yes, we sure do." Then she took Elise's hands in hers. "Now, darling, tell me the truth, do I really look bloated?"

Theo looked in the mirror at Ginger's Bayou Beauties and winced. "It's too short."

Ginger cooed and purred, her big, bright red hair curling around her cherubic face. Flashing her big brown eyes, she giggled. "Tee-do, you look so handsome. Why if I didn't have a steady boyfriend, you'd be in serious trouble."

Theo glanced from Ginger's beaming face to Elise's blank one. Hard to read, that cool little blonde. She'd been mighty quiet on the short ride into the village. And she'd been ultra-lady-like since they'd arrived at Ginger's.

"What do you think?" he asked Elise now, his gaze touching on hers in the mirror's reflection.

"You look much better," Elise said. Her tone told him she was distracted. Or plotting how to torture him next.

"You don't seem too impressed by my handiwork, suga'," Ginger said on a long, drawn-out whine. "What's the matter, Elise? He doesn't look like all those preppy boys you date up in Shreveport."

"He looks just fine," Elise said, her voice like ice water dripping off a cypress limb. "Thank you, Ginger."

Ginger took the charge card Elise handed her, frowned, then went about adding up the cost of the haircut.

Theo got out of the chair, feeling the warm air from the overhead heating vent on his freshly shaven neck. "What's eating at you?" he asked Elise.

She refused to look at him. "Oh, nothing. I'm just worried about *Grand-mère*. She's saying things that don't make any sense to me."

"Your grandmother is as sharp as a tack," Theo said, grinning. "She has the energy of someone half her age."

"Yes, too much energy," Elise countered. "Her mind is always moving ahead. But she has some strange notions these days."

"Want to talk about it?"

"No."

He watched as she signed the charge receipt. Thanking Ginger again, Elise headed for the door.

"You come back anytime, Tee-do," Ginger said, her smile full of appreciation.

"Thanks," Theo said, glad he had the excuse of being Maggie's intended to shield him from the likes of Ginger St. James. Remembering that Maggie might no longer be his, Theo felt a tug of regret. Maybe he should just tell Elise this was pointless. Maggie wouldn't even return his phone calls.

He glanced over at her, saw the haughty way she carried herself to her little sports car, and decided even though he was being tortured with new haircuts and such, he was still enjoying himself way too much to stop this silly notion.

In another week or so, it would all be over anyway. Elise would go back to her job at Melancon Oil and Gas in Shreveport, and he'd go back to helping his family try to make ends meet.

Until then, Theo would just have to make the best of this awkward situation. And who knew, maybe Maggie would see him in a different light if he did clean up and try to better himself.

Maybe.

Maybe he wanted that still.

He looked over at Elise, and wondered if maybe he no longer had eyes for Maggie Aguillard after all.

# CHAPTER SEVEN

"What does it matter which fork I eat with?" Theo asked, his pulse quickening with anger at having to endure this, and excitement at having Elise so close.

She was showing him how to eat at a formal table. He was ignoring the placement of the silverware, and instead watching the way her hair fell across her neck and face as she leaned over to put the dessert spoon over the Spode Christmas china.

"It's just the way things are," Elise said, her smile warm. "It's silly, but necessary, I suppose."

"Well, why is it so necessary. One mouth, one fork. That works just fine for me."

She gave him an indulgent smile. "But we'll have several different courses for our formal Christmas dinner. If you want to impress Maggie, just remember not to use your dessert spoon for your soup or gumbo."

Theo heard her intent loud and clear. This was all about Maggie. Yesterday, he'd endured a haircut at Ginger's, then a fitting at some fancy men's store on Canal Street in New Orleans. He'd endured and enjoyed being with Elise the whole time. She was smart and funny and sensitive and…beautiful. On the way home, they'd laughed and talked about everything from art to baseball. Thankfully, Theo knew a bit about both. He thought Elise had been pleasantly surprised that he did. This was supposed to be all about Maggie, but Theo wanted badly to impress Elise Melancon, too.

"It's awfully kind of you to help me like this, Elise. But what if Maggie doesn't even notice?"

"Then you will at least be able to manage your way through your first formal dinner at *Belle Terre*," she replied with a smug satisfaction. "And I will be the proud teacher. Manners will help you through the worst of situations, Theo."

Well, at least she was in a better mood today. Yesterday, she'd been downright hard to talk to at times. Not that it was easy for Theo to talk to her on any given day. But he wasn't ready to give up completely. He'd finally had her laughing and chatting by the end of their time together yesterday. And he liked her that way.

But he didn't like having to learn this ridiculous dining ritual. "Why do I have to have a dinner plate and a salad plate. At home, we mostly just eat everything off the same plate."

"That's fine for everyday," Elise said, her tone patient and low-key. "But for a formal dinner party, it's important to have a plate or bowl for each course. And we haven't even gotten to the finger bowl yet."

Theo lifted his head. "There's a bowl for my fingers?"

"To wash up," she replied, then indicated with her own fingers dancing in the air. "In case you've eaten shellfish or something sticky or messy."

"Oh, you mean like a mudbug," he said, referring to one of the mainstays of his income, the crawfish. "We just go down to the swamp and wash up there. Sometimes I just let the 'gators lick that spicy mess right off my hands."

"You are such a tease," she said, shaking her head.

"Me, I'm thinking you've never been messy a day in your life," he replied, his nose following the sweet floral scent of her hair.

"I've been known to play in the dirt," she said with a little grin.

"Oh, and when was the last time you played in the dirt, or mud, or got caught in the rain?" Theo said as he watched her toying with a salad fork.

She had long, slender fingers and pretty pink fingernails. She wore only one ring, a dainty thing with a tiny little diamond in the center. Not exactly what he would have expected a wealthy socialite to wear. "Where'd you get the ring?"

Elise followed his eyes to her left hand, then smiled. "It was *Grand-mère*'s. She gave it to me on my sixteenth birthday. It's got a lot of sentimental value. My grandfather Jacques gave it to her when they were first in love."

Theo saw the love and appreciation in her eyes. For all her airs, Elise really was a down-to-earth kind of woman.

"Okay, now answer my original question. When was the last time you got caught in the rain?"

She lifted her eyebrows, frowning. "I got caught in the rain about three weeks ago, leaving work."

"Leaving Melancon Oil and Gas in lovely downtown Shreveport?"

"Yes. How did you know I work there?"

"Your *grand-mère* likes to brag about how smart you are."

That statement brought that worried, cloudy look to her pretty eyes.

"You do like your job with the company, right?"

She nodded, than sat down on the Chippendale chair next to him, her pretty black pleated skirt falling softly around her legs. "Yes, I do. But *Mamere* has other ideas. Has she mentioned anything to you about starting a new department at Melancon, here closer to home?"

Theo turned his head sideways and gave her a quizzical look. "Now why would your *grand-mère* mention things about her business to the likes of *moi?*"

"I know she tells you things," Elise said, her tone almost defensive. "She has this notion of starting an environmental and ecological department, with both of us working there from what I can gather."

Theo couldn't believe what he was hearing. Betty Jean had mentioned this very idea to him many, many times. She'd also promised him a position in her company, in that very department, but she'd never mentioned that her granddaughter might be a part of it. Said she'd take him on without his degree, as long as he finished up school in the meantime. But he didn't dare tell Elise that. She'd go into a tizzy, for sure. Plus he'd never actually taken Betty Jean seriously. Maybe he should now.

"Your grandmother is always talking about dis and dat, I mean, this and that," he said, acutely aware of his enunciation. And acutely aware of the woman next to him.

"Oh, never mind," Elise said, getting up to spin around like a ballerina. "I think we're done for today. At least, you should be able to get through dinner by just remembering to start at the outside and work your way in, with the silverware. Watching *Grand-mère* and me will take care of the rest."

"Now that part I can enjoy," he said, grinning. "Watching you, I mean."

She frowned again, then blushed. "Well, the main thing you need to watch is all that charm, Theo."

Suddenly, Theo had had enough of all this fancy stuff, but he had more than enough charm to last the rest of the day. "Okay, then, if we're done with the *formal* part of our work, how 'bout I take over?"

"And do what?" she asked, her voice going all soft and unsure.

Theo took that as a good sign. "It's a surprise, *chère*."

"I don't like surprises."

"You'll like this one. I just want to thank you, for helping me out." To emphasize that this was strictly gratitude, even though he hoped it would change into something else, he added, "Maggie won't know what hit her when I walk in all gussied up and knowing which fork to use."

That seemed to bring a steely determination back into Elise's eyes. "Okay, I guess we've worked hard today. And tomorrow we go into New Orleans to pick up your suit. My grandfather's personal tailor promised he'd have it altered just right."

"You sure are pretty when you're all business," Theo said, loving the way her creamy skin changed to peachy when she got flustered.

"Stop staring at me, please."

"I like to look at you. You're like this little *catin,* like fine porcelain."

"I'm not a doll," she said, her guard up again. "And we have to keep this strictly professional."

"It's not like I'm paying you or anything—it's just an agreement between friends, *oui?* Can't we at least pretend to like each other."

"I do like you," she said, then she brought a hand to her throat to touch on those infernal pearls she always wore. "I mean, you seem like a nice man, Theo."

"But a gentleman doesn't stare, right?"

She pushed at her hair. "Exactly. It's rather rude."

"I'm a rather rude person at times."

"If you keep this up, I won't be able to enjoy this surprise you've planned."

"Okay, then, I won't stare anymore. Will you come with me and trust me in this?"

"Can I trust you?"

"I'm learning to behave. I'm trying real hard to be a gentleman for you."

She looked up at him, shock registering on her face

in a delicate sheen. "You're doing this for Maggie, remember?"

"Maggie who?" he said, grinning.

Elise wasn't sure what to expect next. Theo was that kind of man. Full of surprises. Yesterday, he'd surprised her in New Orleans by talking all about the history of that interesting city. Theo knew things about the history of New Orleans that Elise had never taken the time to learn. And he knew about art. They'd strolled by the gallery with the famous Blue Dog paintings hanging for all to see. Theo knew all about the dog in the paintings—a Catahoula hound. And he knew everything about the artist, too. He could identify antiques as well as plants and animals, all with that wicked grin on his face. He had a quick wit that showed his intelligence, when he wanted to show it, that is.

Then today, he'd surprised her yet again by insisting he had to work extra hard to make sure everything her grandmother had hired him to do got done. Only after that had he agreed to sit down in the dining room and go over proper table etiquette.

And now he had her in a pirogue and they were moving through the still waters of the bayou. He'd told her to bundle up, they might be late getting back to the big house.

And she had no idea where he was taking her.

"It's beautiful," Elise said as Theo guided the small canoelike boat through the green waters.

Cypress trees draped with Spanish moss hung over a swamp that was covered with palmetto bushes, briars, vines and saplings. The air was crisp and chilly, but every now and then a ray of soft sunlight would hit her on the face, bringing a bit of warm to the nippy afternoon.

"We'll get warmed up when we get there," Theo said, noting the way she huddled in her wool wrap. "My *maman* should be there already. She'll have some hot cocoa, for sure."

"I'm okay," she said, glad to hear his mother would be their chaperone. "I've just never been this far into the swamp." And she wondered why she was doing so now, with this mysterious man. Then she watched him on the seat in front of her. His hair was clipped and layered, but it was still long enough to lift around his ears and forehead as the wind played through it. It shimmered to a rich coffee brown in the scant sunlight. His powerful arms pushed with a kind of elegant strength and grace against the current, as he lifted the oars in and out of the water in a timeless, symmetric way. He wore a long-sleeved cotton sweater and faded jeans.

Elise had to admit he looked pretty good, even without the tailored suit. She could only imagine how nice he'd look when the suit was finished.

Maggie Aguillard had sure been a lucky girl. Why had she broken up with Theo?

Stop that, Elise told herself. You are fulfilling an obligation to your grandmother. It would have been petty and disrespectful to do anything else.

"Did your *maman* question where we were headed?" Theo asked, bringing Elise out of her silent admonishments.

"Mother, oh, she was off to an afternoon tea at one of her sorority sister's homes just down the river. She'll be gone for hours. Daddy's golfing at the country club with his lawyer friends. And then tonight some of the others start arriving. No one will even miss me."

"Did you tell your *mamere* you were spending the afternoon with me?"

"Of course," Elise replied, wondering why he was so concerned. "*Mamere* said to have a good time."

Come to think of it, Betty Jean had been beaming, her smile full of serenity and confidence. But then, her grandmother had been beaming the whole time Elise had been home. Her grandmother was so happy that her entire family would be here for Christmas.

Elise thought about the busy pace of the holidays, then listened to the sounds of the swamp. The soft sway of the water, the gentle pull of a crisp December wind, the sounds of animals scurrying away through the duckweeds and water reeds. In spite of wondering where Theo was taking her, she had to admit it was nice and peaceful here, giving one pause to reflect.

*Thank You, Lord, for allowing me to have a good life. Thank You for my dear grandmother, and* Grand-père *up in heaven now. Thank You for dying for my sins.*

The silent prayer felt good, felt right. Elise glanced up at Theo. He was watching the way ahead of them, which made her feel completely safe for some strange reason.

"You okay back there, *chère?*"

"I'm fine."

"What's going on in that head of yours?"

Should she tell him she'd just said a prayer. Why not? Theo was a Christian. She knew that. "I was giving thanks to the Lord, for such a good family and for my dear grandparents."

Theo halted the pirogue for a minute, then turned to look at her, a gentle stirring in his dark eyes. "That's very sweet, you know."

Elise felt tears pricking at her eyes. "Christmas is such a special time."

"No time is more special."

"You feel it, too, then?"

"The presence of Christ, here in this water?"

"Yes."

"*Oui,* I always feel closer to God out here in this bayou. He made the heavens and the earth. It's up to us to protect it, and to show Him we can take care of it."

Elise thought of her grandmother's wishes for her to start a new life here on the bayou.

To help protect this good, green earth.

*I don't understand, Lord,* she silently said. *Why me, why now?*

Then she looked up at Theo and she saw the flare of that something there in his dark eyes, something good and positive and pure and gentle.

And she wondered if God had a plan for them, here, together at *Belle Terre.*

# CHAPTER EIGHT

"What is this place?" Elise asked as Theo banked the pirogue near a small wooden dock. She stared up at the small cabin that sat like a square brown pelican on stilts high above the flowing waters of the dark bayou.

"Dis is where my papa was born," Theo replied, his tone quiet and full of reverence. "And his daddy before him. Dis is the first cabin ever built by a Galliano. It's been here for over a century."

"But it looks so clean and tidy," Elise said as he helped her out of the boat. "I mean, it looks brand-new."

"That's because I've been fixing it up, for my daddy. He's been so down lately, what with not being able to work and all. I wanted to give him a special Christmas present."

"You did this?" Elise asked, her gaze moving from the tiny cabin in front of them to the man beside her.

"I did indeed. Been working on it off and on since summer. It's finished now, except for one thing."

"What's that?" she asked, gaining a new respect for this man.

From the cabin door, they heard his mother calling. Elise glanced up to find a plump, dark-headed woman grinning down at them. "Tee-do, hurry you up and bring that pretty *catin* in here outta the cold, you hear?"

Theo waved to his mother. "Coming, *Maman.*" Then he turned back to Elise. "I want to decorate the Christmas tree, for my papa. And I want you to help me."

Touched that he wanted her to be a part of this, Elise looked up at him. "Theo, that is so sweet. But shouldn't Maggie be the one—"

He looked to where his robust mother stood waiting. "I don't want to talk about Maggie right now."

"Don't you want to wait for her to come home in case you two work things out?"

She watched as he looked away, his expression turning sheepish and unsure. "She won't be home until Christmas Eve and I want it to be ready before then. But if you feel uncomfortable—"

"No, no. I'll be glad to help you," Elise replied, feeling the duel battle of guilt and impropriety taking over her soul. But was it so inappropriate for a friend to help another friend? She'd already helped Theo with improving himself. How could she turn down this latest request? And besides, his mother was here to keep them both in check.

"Let's get started," she told him.

He nodded, seemingly relieved. "Okay, then. Let's get inside out of this afternoon chill."

But Elise wondered if she *was* doing the right thing, being here with Theo. *I'm very confused, Lord. Help me to sort through these feelings I'm beginning to have for this man.*

She had to stay focused and objective. And she had to keep reminding herself that Theo might once again belong with another woman.

Theo wondered why he'd thought it such a grand idea to hang around Elise Melancon. He should just tell her the truth, that he didn't miss Maggie so very much. He shouldn't have agreed to this idea, but he'd only done it to please her dear grandmother, whom he respected and cherished like his own family.

*I've made a big mess, Lord,* he prayed. *And I need You to help me straighten things out.*

But how, Theo wondered. How could he tell Elise the truth without hurting her? His feelings for her had changed somewhere between the forced haircut and the reality of getting to know her better. Or maybe, truth be told, his feelings had *begun* the minute he'd seen her standing there with her grandmother. Only now, he could never tell her that. She would leave *Belle Terre* thinking his heart belonged to another.

"What's wrong?" Elise asked him now as she gazed up at him. They were standing on the porch of the cabin and she was obviously waiting for him to introduce her to his mother.

"Dat boy got his head in de clouds," Theo's mother said, laughing. "I'm Deidre. I gave birth to this big oaf."

Theo watched to see if Elise was put off by his formidable mother's chuckling and clucking. But he should have known Elise Melancon would never show disdain—that would be impolite.

"Hello," Elise said, taking the hand the other woman extended. "It's so nice to meet you, Mrs. Galliano."

"Call me Deidre, honey," she said, grasping Elise's hand in hers with a sturdy shake. Theo knew her hands must feel work-worn and rough, but the warmth of her touch couldn't be denied. He hoped Elise would like his mother.

Echoing Elise's earlier words to him, Deidre held on to Elise as she gave him a quizzical motherly look. "What's the matter with you, boy?"

"Nothing," he said. "Just thinking."

Deidre chuckled again. "You know what I say— thinking too much can only lead a man to trouble."

Elise laughed, too. "Your mother sounds like a smart woman."

That made Theo grin. "She is. She'd have to be to put with her brood of children."

"Ain't dat the truth, for sure," Deidre said as she tugged Elise to the door. "C'mon in here and see what my oldest son's been up to."

"I'd like to meet the rest of your family sometime," Elise said to Theo, then she glanced away, as if embarrassed.

"Someday," Theo replied, wondering if she'd ever get that chance. And wondering if he'd ever get a chance to explain his actions to Elise. It didn't help that his mother was giving him intense and questioning stares. "Right now, we need to get this cabin decorated for Papa."

He opened the screened door, then the thick cypress door of the tiny two room cabin. "I'll light the lamp," he said as the women followed him inside. "There isn't any electricity in here."

Theo went to a kerosene lamp sitting on the small kitchen table that his grandfather had built by hand. After putting a lighter to the thick charred wick, he turned at Elise's gasp.

"Oh, my," she said, spinning around, her arms held out wide. "Theo, this is just lovely."

"My *bébé* boy's done a very good job," Deidre said, beaming.

Theo grinned with pride. He'd refurbished the cabin with as many authentic pieces as he could find. "I shopped the antique stores in New Orleans and up in Lafayette," he said, shrugging. "And I even found some of this stuff at estate sales, some tossed out on the road."

Deidre's dark eyes went from her son's face to Elise's. "Me, I'm thinking I need to go to the truck and find that basket of snacks I packed. I made cocoa."

Theo waved her away. She'd insisted on coming to help, but he knew she had just wanted to get a glimpse of rich, pretty Elise Melancon, too. At least his endearing mother had the good sense to give them some privacy.

"Oh, it's a shame to think people would just toss out their heritage," Elise said as she moved her hand over the shining veneer of a primitive pie safe. "I think it's very noble of you to want to preserve an important part of your past."

Theo nodded. "I guess that's what your *grand-mère* is trying to do, with *Belle Terre*."

He watched as Elise's expression turned thoughtful. "Yes, I suppose so. Maybe that's why she's so bent on creating this new division at Melancon Oil and Gas."

"It would be a good thing," Theo said. "The oil companies have put a big dent in these old wetlands. Oil and gas are necessary, I realize. But we still need to leave the land as we find it and hurt not the earth nor the sea, as the Bible tells us."

Elise turned to face him, her eyes glowing in the muted light from the lamp. "A lot of damage has been done, what with draining and dredging and building the oil and gas canals. I wouldn't know where to begin to make things right."

"Well, your *grand-mère* has the right idea, that's for sure. Trying to clean up some of the damage would be a good start. I hope I can be a part of that someday."

She came to stand beside him as he opened a shuttered window. When he turned to face her, the waning sunlight hit on her flaxen hair, making it shimmer like gold dust. "Do you think I should consider *Grand-mère's* request for me to head up this new department?"

Theo didn't know how to answer that. If Elise agreed to this, it would mean she'd be back here at *Belle Terre,* a lot. It would mean he'd get to see her. A lot. It would also mean he needed to level with her right now, no matter what the future held. "I think that is something you have to decide within your own heart," he replied, hoping that weak answer would be enough for now.

Elise gave him a quizzical look, then nodded. "Well, we'd better get that tree decorated before it gets dark out there. I don't think I'm ready to spend the night in the swamp."

"No worries there," Theo replied, glad to change the subject. "Your *maman* will have my hide if I keep you out too long. It wouldn't look right, even if my *maman* is here to keep me in line."

He saw the speculative look Elise cast toward him. Was she thinking that they didn't look right together, in the swamp or out in the real world, either way?

Just another reminder that he was way in over his head, Theo decided.

The little tree was tiny. It hadn't taken them long to string the strands of popcorn Theo had brought along. After that, they put some handmade decorations on the small cedar tree. The gleaming white Chrismon symbols only reinforced the closeness Elise was finding to the Lord, being back here in Bayou Branche. The white dove, the chalice, the crown, the star of David, and all the other symbols reminded her of what being a true Christian was really all about.

When they finished, she stood back to sip the hot cocoa Theo's mother had brought in a big Thermos. "It's lovely," she stated, happy with their handiwork. Deidre had gone outside again, to piddle with the porch decorations.

"Beautiful," Theo said, but when Elise glanced over at him, he wasn't looking at the tree. Instead, his dark eyes were moving over her face with a tender intensity that left

Elise feeling all warm and cozy inside. Maybe it was just the rich hot cocoa his mother had insisted they drink.

"You're staring again," she said to break the silence.

"I know."

"You can't stare at Maggie like that. You might scare her away again."

"Do I scare *you?*"

Elise had to think about that. She couldn't answer him with her honest feelings. Yes, he scared her. But it was in a nice, exciting kind of way. "You intrigue me," she finally said. "I wish I had time to really know you and understand you, Theo."

"Nothing much to me, *chère*," he replied, his eyes still on her as he leaned back against the table. "I'm a very simple man. I just want a good, decent life, a faith-filled life here in this place where I was born and raised. I just want to belong, and in belonging, I want to contribute, to give back something, anything."

"You do belong," Elise said, her heart doing strange tap-dancing things. "You belong here."

"Maybe you do, too."

It sounded like an invitation, or maybe a challenge.

She put down her cup and turned away. "Lately, I'm not so sure where I belong. I thought I had everything life could offer me. A good job with my daddy's company, a nice home, good friends to laugh and have fun with."

"Do you have a special friend? A man you're interested in?"

She looked at the twinkling decorations on the tiny little tree. "No. I've dated various men on and off, but there's no one special. I envy what you have with Maggie. I mean, the way you've gone to such trouble to try to impress and get her back. It shows you care about her feelings."

"I care," he said. Then he looked away, too. "I've always cared. But I've also learned that two people don't always make it on feelings alone. It takes more. It takes a commitment. They have to both want the same things."

"Does Maggie want the simple life you mentioned?" Elise asked. She had to know. She didn't want to see Theo get hurt if Maggie rejected him.

"I don't know," he said. "Reckon we'll find out if she takes me back, *oui?*" Then he took their empty cups and packed them back inside the insulated picnic bag his mother had brought. "We'd better get back. It's getting cold out there."

Elise waited as he bundled her wool wrap around her shoulders. Why wouldn't he look at her again?

"Theo?" she asked, afraid he was mad at her for asking him such personal questions.

He finally looked up at her, his big hands still on her arms over the warmth of her gray shawl. "Don't ask me any more questions, Elise. Not now."

"I'm sorry," she said, "I didn't mean to pry."

He backed up, his hands falling at his side. "I don't mind so much. It's just—"

He didn't finish. Instead, he turned and headed for the door. "Let's get back."

Outside Elise said goodbye to his mother. Deidre gave

her a hug, patting her on the back. "It was good to meet you, *bebelle.*"

The ride through the dusk-hued swamp was subdued. Elise studied the giant cypress trees along the bank, watching the way their pretty branches swayed in the soft, cold wind. Underneath, clusters of palmetto branches stood stark and scattered, like knife blades twisted between the dark mud and clumps of briars. This place was timeless, a true gift from the Lord.

She looked from the trees to the man guiding the boat. He was as much a part of this bayou as those old trees.

And suddenly, Elise wanted to belong somewhere, too, just as Theo did. She wanted to belong here, right here, with this man. Because she had fallen in love with Theo Galliano.

# CHAPTER NINE

"It's my turn again," Theo told Elise the next afternoon.

They were sitting in the back den at *Belle Terre,* where they'd just had a lively discussion with Betty Jean regarding everything from politics to potluck dinners. Tired but also obviously invigorated, by the way her green eyes had shined, Betty Jean had gone upstairs to rest before dinner.

"But we're not finished," Elise said, thinking with pride that Theo had held his own with her keen grandmother. "We haven't gone over the difference between semi-formal and black tie."

Theo leaned close, giving her another one of those sideways looks of his. The kind of look that made her heart go crazy and her mind go reeling.

"I think I can figure that out, *chère.* Semi-formal means you kinda need to get all dolled up, more like church clothes, and black-tie speaks for itself, *oui?* Wear something black, mebbe the tie?"

She laughed, seeing the teasing light in his eyes. "Okay, I guess I'm being a bit too overbearing here, but what if Maggie and you have a chance to attend some of the Mardi Gras events after Christmas. You'd need to know what to wear."

"I don't do events."

"And why not?"

He sighed, rubbed a hand down the five-o'clock shadow on his face. "Because I'm a Cajun, Elise. I like a good old-fashioned *boucherie* instead of some fancy party."

"You'd rather attend a pig roast with Maggie than a social event that could help you in both your career and your personal life?"

"I'd rather attend a pig roast with *you,* just to show you that everything in life isn't about seeing and being seen, suga'. Sometimes, it's just about being with family and friends—real friends, the kind you know you can count on for the rest of your life, not just until the next deal goes down."

Elise felt the sting of that implication. "I suppose you think all of my so-called friends are just as shallow and petty as I seem to you."

"Ah, now, don't go pouting on me," he said as he slouched down beside her on the couch. "Elise, smile for me."

She pouted, crossing her arms and giving him a very cold shoulder.

But Theo knew how to charm her. He got closer to her, then put his arm around her. He leaned his head on her shoulder, then whispered in her ear. "C'mon, smile for me, *chère*. Just one little bitty pretty Elise smile. You know that smile can light up a cloudy day."

That cold shoulder suddenly became very warm. Elise could feel that sensational warmth moving through her entire system, like the first winds of spring after a cold, cold winter. But she didn't smile for him just yet. "I won't apologize for who I am, Theo. And it hurts me that you can't see inside, to the real me."

"Why does it hurt?" he asked, his breath fanning her hair, his hand across her back heavy with both security and mystery.

She wanted to tell him it hurt because instead of wanting to reform him, she just wanted to be with him, and she wanted to *impress him*. Just him. The real man. The man she'd fallen for. She didn't need to change Theo. She liked him just fine the way he was. But she couldn't tell him that. He'd probably laugh in her face.

"It just upsets me that you think I'm such a horrible person."

He turned her head with a tanned hand on her hair, his dark eyes roaming over her face. "I don't think you're horrible. I think you are a sweet, good girl, Elise. And you're sure pretty. But we do come from very different worlds."

She thought about that, about how they'd lived on the same land and never even known each other. "Worlds apart, and yet you've been right here all the time."

He pried one of her hands away from the tight grip she had them twisted in. "*Oui*, I've been right here all along. And dat right dere ought to tell you where we stand. You didn't even know I existed until your *grand-mère* pointed it out to you."

"So you intend to hold that against me forever?"

"*Non,* I don't intend to hold that against you at all. And I'm sorry if I seemed to be putting you down. Will you forgive me for being so impolite?" When she still didn't respond, he rolled his eyes and said, "I'm an just a big ol' oaf."

That made her smile. "You are a big ol' clown."

He chuckled. "This clown loves to see you smile."

Elise's eyes locked with his as the smile died on her face. He was so close, she could see the black of his beautiful irises. It was as if she were looking into the very depths of the deepest swamp. She thought she'd surely drown in all that mysterious darkness.

"How do you really feel about me, Theo?" She had to understand what was brewing between them. Maybe she was just imagining it. Maybe he didn't feel anything for her. At least he shouldn't. He loved Maggie. But Maggie left him.

"You really want to know that?"

She nodded, her heart beating with a solid, steady need.

"I feel like this." He leaned close, pulled her into his arms and kissed her.

Elise melted into his touch. Theo Galliano was kissing her, right here in her grandmother's den, with all the world and several newly arrived relatives to see if they happened to walk in. But she couldn't stop him, couldn't stop herself. This felt like the belonging she'd longed for. This felt like she'd become a part of something so good and right that she had to believe the heavens were truly involved. And she thanked God for granting her this feeling, this hope.

Theo seemed to feel the same. His touch was so soft and sure, Elise forgot that kissing him was wrong. She didn't think about lingering feelings he had for Maggie. Somewhere, in the far recesses of her mind, she was glad he and Maggie had broken up.

She thought she heard thunder.

But that turned out to be her mother's well-heeled foot stomping against the hardwood floor. "What in the world do you think you're doing to my little girl?"

Elise felt herself being bodily lifted from Theo's embrace as her mother showed surprising strength with the yanking of her scrawny hand across the neck of Elise's sweater. "Get up!"

"Mother!" Elise said, rising in pure mortification to face her angry, shocked mother. "Stop it."

"No, you two stop it," Cissie said, one foot still patting the floor as she went into a nervous tizzy full of motherly wrath and protection. "I don't know what's going on around here, but I will not tolerate *you* touching my daughter."

Theo stood, too, the look in his eyes mirroring what Cissie was saying. "You're right to be angry, Mrs. Melancon. I don't have any business touching your daughter. I am very sorry."

With that, he turned in a straight-backed stalk and left the room. Elise heard the front door slamming shut.

It felt as if he'd just shut the door on her heart, too.

\* \* \*

"She refuses to come down to dinner," Cissie announced just outside Elise's bedroom door in a voice so loud, Elise heard it very clearly from her room. "Honestly, I don't know what's gotten into that young lady. She won't even consider dating Jason Pilcher anymore. And he's a very nice boy—comes from one of the oldest families in Louisiana—and with all that money—he inherited a vast fortune when his grandfather died, you know. I declare I don't understand why she'd be kissing that…that Cajun." Elise heard a long sigh. "It's just so unseemly. We've raised her to behave herself, to always hold her head up high. She's a Melancon, after all."

Then Elise heard another voice. "You go on down with the others, dear. I'll see if I can talk to her."

Her grandmother! Elise couldn't face her, not yet.

But Betty Jean Melancon didn't let a closed, locked door stop her. "Elise, open this door right now. You hear me, Boo. I need to talk to you."

"I'm not feeling well, *Mamere,*" Elise called out. "Please tell the others I'm sorry."

"No, I'm the one who's sorry," Betty Jean said. "And we need to talk."

Elise heard the gentle plea in her grandmother's words. She couldn't ignore that. Getting up from the wing chair where she'd been sitting by the window since the awful scene downstairs, Elise walked to the door. "Come in, *Mamere.*"

Betty Jean entered the room, wearing a cream dinner dress and her favorite three-strand pearls. Her eyes widened when she looked at Elise. "Are you all right, darling?"

"No," Elise said, her lips trembling with tears she didn't want to shed. "I'm a grown woman, yet I feel as if I'm still seven years old. Mother embarrassed me to no end down there!"

"Come here," her grandmother said, opening her arms wide.

Elise ran to those comforting arms, remembering other hurts and other hugs. *Grand-mère* would know what to do. *Grand-mère* always knew what to do.

"I didn't mean for this to happen," Elise said, her words muffled by cream wool as the scent of White Shoulders lifted from her grandmother's soft arms.

"Neither did I," Betty Jean said, patting Elise's hair. "I shouldn't have asked this of you. It was wrong. So wrong."

Elise pulled away, upset to see the distress in her dear grandmother's eyes. She'd brought that pain. Elise could deal with her own pain, but not her grandmother's. "I've let you down," she said, stepping away to grab a tissue from a nearby table.

Betty Jean slumped into a chair, a sure sign that she was upset. Her grandmother never slumped. "No, Boo, I'm the one who's failed. I didn't see this coming in quite such a way. I mean, I thought—"

"You thought you could depend on me, that you could trust me," Elise said, falling down on the dainty burgundy brocade bench at the end of the tester bed. "You asked me to do one thing and I messed up that one thing so badly."

"Hush up," Betty Jean said. "No real harm has been done. So you kissed Theo. My goodness, that is not a crime in the state of Louisiana."

"But Mother had to go and make such a scene," Elise said, anger overriding her hurt. "Theo left in a huff and everyone, *Mamere,* the whole family, heard her screaming at the top of her lungs."

"The woman has a set of lungs, I'll give her that," said Betty Jean, a glimmer of her wit returning to her watery eyes. "I sure wish I'd seen the look on her face—"

"*Grand-mère,* this isn't funny."

"I'm not laughing, dear. But your mother's rantings are the least of my concerns. I'm more worried about you. You did nothing wrong, Boo. Except maybe kissed the man you've fallen in love with."

Elise sat straight up. "How can you tell that?"

"I'm your grandmother," Betty Jean said with a shrug. "And you are so like me. I remember when I first knew I was in love with your grandfather. Of course, my parents objected immediately. And openly. Just as your mother did today. But that all turned out fine in the end."

Elise smiled at the memory of her dear grandfather, Jacques. "I wish things could turn out fine now, but Theo and I, we shouldn't even be having such thoughts. He was in love with Maggie not too long ago. I'm sure he still is, isn't he?"

"Has he talked about her with you? Has he actually told you he still loves her?"

Elise thought back over the last week and all the conversations she'd had with Theo. They'd talked about manners and etiquette. They'd talked about family and faith. They'd covered art and culture and politics and good books and the kind of music they enjoyed.

And all the while, she'd always been the one to bring up Maggie. She'd been the one to assume that Theo still loved Maggie, that he was doing this to please Maggie, to hopefully get things straight with her.

"Boo, you haven't answered my question," her grandmother said, a hand on her arm.

Elise looked over at her grandmother, realization making her heart hammer in an erratic fashion. "No, *Mamere,* now that I think about it, Theo has never once said he still loves Maggie. In fact, he barely mentions her unless I bring up her name."

Betty Jean lowered her head, her eyebrows lifting. "Don't you find that rather odd, dear?"

"Very odd indeed," Elise replied. "And I intend to find out why."

"That's more like it," Betty Jean said, getting up with a spry quickness, her smile intact again.

Elise turned to give her grandmother a quizzical look. "You seem too pleased about this, *Mamere.*"

"Of course, I'm pleased," Betty Jean said, her eyes completely innocent, her smile practiced and steady. "I can't bear to see you in tears, darling. And now you're not crying anymore."

"No, I'm not," Elise said, a new determination making her stand up straight. "I'll be down to dinner in just a minute. I seem to have regained my appetite."

Betty Jean clasped her hands together. "As I said, just like me."

Elise watched as her happy grandmother left the room.

"Too much like you, I imagine," Elise said. "Way too much."

# CHAPTER TEN

"Let me see if I understand this," Cissie said two days later.

It was Christmas Eve and the whole gang had arrived the night before. The men and boys were off on the traditional Christmas Eve bird hunt. Elise and her mother were sitting at the table in the garden room, having a quick breakfast before they dived into the rest of the holiday cooking. Later that night, they'd all go to the Christmas Eve candlelight services at church, then return here for a casual dinner and the opening of one present each.

"Your grandmother asked you to 'tutor' this man in time for Christmas. To teach him manners and how to be a proper gentleman so he could win back his girlfriend, who's coming to dinner here tomorrow night?"

"Yes, Mother, that's right," Elise said, careful to keep her tone calm and reserved. She wouldn't cause a scene, not with her mother, nor with Theo. That is, whenever she had a chance to see Theo again.

He'd been avoiding her.

"Well, the man obviously hasn't learned too many manners. He should know that kissing one woman while he's trying to impress another one is simply bad form."

"It was a mistake, Mother," Elise said, thinking in her heart that kissing Theo had been anything but a mistake. "We got carried away. I know it was wrong, and it won't happen again."

"I'm sure it won't, and you really should just nip this in the bud right now by refusing to go anywhere near that man again. In fact, I'll tell Reginald to make sure he seats you two as far away from each other tomorrow night as possible."

"I think that's a very good idea," Elise said, too heart-sick to argue with her mother. "Besides, as soon as Maggie shows up, Theo will only have eyes for her."

Cissie dropped her fork to stare over at her daughter. "That's as it should be, darling. I can understand how you might develop a little crush on that man. I mean, he is handsome in a diamond-in-the-rough kind of way. But those bad-boy types can lead to no good. And you deserve better. You have to remember who you are, Elise. You are a Melancon."

Elise shook her head and threw down her napkin. "And being a Melancon means that I have to be proper and above reproach at all times, right, Mother?"

"Yes, that's exactly what it means," Cissie said, her blue eyes flaming. "You have to think of your image, Elise. Of the company's good name."

"That same image, that same good name that has

helped pollute this very land?" Elise said, getting up to stalk toward the kitchen. "Right now, Mother, I'm not so sure I'm proud of being a Melancon."

"How can you say that?" Cissie called after her, her hand fluttering in the air. "Elise, I'm not finished talking to you. That man has already turned your head, and against your own family at that. You have to end this, right now."

"It's over already, Mother," Elise said as she grabbed her beige wool topper and headed out the door. "I'm going for a walk."

"It's freezing out there," Cissie said on a long whine.

"I need some fresh air," Elise said over her shoulder.

"No, you need to have your head examined," her mother shouted. "And so does your grandmother, if you ask me."

"Maybe we do at that," Elise said under her breath.

Theo *felt* her coming even before he saw her. He was that in tune to Elise Melancon. So in tune that he'd made the fatal mistake of kissing her. And wishing he could kiss her again.

He turned from where he'd been pruning winter-dead branches from the boxwood hedges that lined the white wooden fence around the perimeters of the vast estate. Turned and took a breath as his heart began to hurt with a pain that didn't seem familiar.

She looked so pretty, all bundled up in beige, with a red wool scarf tucked around her neck. She was wearing jeans and expensive low-heeled, pointy-toed leather boots the same rich beige color of her coat. Her flaxen-colored hair lifted out in the crisp morning wind like silken wheat. Her cheeks were a bright pink. Her expression bordered on petulant, but she had a look of resolve about her.

He loved her.

Theo accepted that fact and let it rush over him with the same gentle force as the cool wind. He closed his eyes, said a quick prayer for direction, and took in the contrasting warmth of the bright morning sun.

When he opened his eyes, she was near and she was looking at him like a fawn caught in the forest, that same realization of love shining brightly in her own eyes.

"Morning," he called, hoping to appear as bland and blank as the white fence behind him.

"Hello," she replied, her eyes glowing with unspoken fears and hopes. "I didn't know you'd be here."

"I didn't plan on being here," he responded, his hedge clippers suddenly heavy in his hands. "Just finishing up some work I've been neglecting."

The cutting edge of that remark caused her to take in her breath. "I guess I've been taking up too much of your time."

"It's okay," he said, turning around to clip tiny dry leaves. Because it felt good to let his rage out in such a sharp, harsh, snippy way. "I picked up my suit yesterday. Fits perfectly."

"I knew it would."

He turned, threw down the clippers, marched toward her and pulled her into his arms. Then he kissed her and this time he made sure it left the right impression. He wanted her to know that he loved her, but he also knew that what he'd done was wrong. He'd woven this tangled web and now it was up to him to untangle things. He never should have agreed to this arrangement.

But when he let go and looked into her eyes, his heart sputtered out of control and went careening off in another direction. "We're in big trouble," he said on a winded breath.

"I know." She backed away and wiped at the moisture in her eyes. "And I don't know what to do about it. I don't want to stop you from getting back together with Maggie."

"I said the suit fits, Elise. That doesn't mean *I* will ever fit. You have to remember that."

She whirled to glare at him. "Because you refuse to fit, Theo. You've already judged me and I'm sure that the way I've acted—the way I've reacted—to you hasn't helped. You must think the worst of me."

He urged her back into his arms, then stroked her hair away from her face. "*Non,* you know what I find? That I'm thinking the best of you. I'm thinking that I could fall for you."

"Stop," she said, pulling away to lean over the fence. All around them, the ancient oaks held sway like protective sentinels, while the squirrels and birds and other forest creatures went about their normal fussy business. "You can't fall for me. I won't allow that to happen."

"Because I'm not good enough?"

"No, because you *are* good enough. Too good. I won't allow you to ruin what you want with Maggie—"

"Leave her out of this."

She looked up at him, her eyes full of questions. "How can I? How can I forget that we started this because of her? And I know by the way you don't like to talk about her that you're trying to do the right thing. You don't even want me to be a part of what you share with Maggie. Isn't that right, Theo? Isn't that why you don't talk much about her? You want what you have with Maggie to stay private."

It was his turn to walk away, to put some distance between them. To put some distance between himself and his guilt. "There is a lot about Maggie and me that I can't talk about," he said, the sick feeling of dread shrouding his soul like a too-warm blanket.

He heard her hand hitting the fence. "You see, that's one of the things I appreciate about you. You are a gentleman, Theo. You *are* a gentleman in all the ways that really count. You're protecting the woman you love. And that means I have no part in your life."

"Does that mean we're done, finished?"

"Yes," she said, the word so soft and final he thought he'd heard her wrong. "I've done my job and I've seen that you don't need instructions on etiquette, or manners, or knowing the right thing to do."

"So that's it then?"

"Yes. That has to be it. I won't come between you and Maggie. It's not right and it would cause too much heartache. I'll see you at dinner tomorrow night."

He heard her boots hitting dirt, knew she was walking away from him for good. He wanted to run to her, assure her that he didn't love Maggie now, tell her the truth, that this had started out as some sort of black joke, his way of getting even with Elise because she was a good girl who brought out the bad in him. But it had turned into something so rich and full of hope that it brought him to his knees with longing. Elise, with all her wholesome goodness, made him want to be good, too.

But he didn't tell her any of those things.

Instead he just turned and watched her walk away.

The house was glowing with the warmth and charm of the holidays. Outside in an open area of the back gardens, a bonfire that Theo had helped build, burned brightly in the night sky. Some of the relatives were gathered around it, sipping hot apple cider and hot chocolate.

Elise stood at one of the big windows in the dining room, the scent of cinnamon and mulberry candles mingling with the rich smell of Reginald's Cajun fried turkey with seafood stuffing. The long mahogany dining table was set with the gold-etched Christmas china. The shimmering light from the antique silver candelabras sitting on each side of the evergreen-and-magnolia leaf centerpiece cast a thousand glistening shadows across the room. The massive sideboard groaned with the weight of three different kinds of bread puddings and pound cakes, pecan pies and decorated sugar cookies. In the great entranceway, the huge tree sparkled with all the ornaments and baubles of her grandmother's life. Ornaments and baubles Elise had helped collect and hang there. She could see the fire from the parlor's great big hearth reflected in the shimmering ornaments.

Everything here is so precious.

Elise turned from the window, closing her eyes as she listened to the sounds of family and home. Her cousins laughing and running in the other rooms, her aunts and uncles moving about in the kitchen, her grandmother's gentle instructions carrying throughout the house and Reginald's reassuring answers, her mother's shrill complaints said in that endearing Southern voice that brought Elise both pain and comfort.

I belong here, she thought, her hand reaching out to touch the velvety red blossoms of a poinsettia placed on a side table. I belong here.

Now, she understood why her grandmother had called them all home. Now, she understood why her grandmother had insisted she help Theo. Now, she understood why her grandmother wanted her to be a real part of Melancon Oil and Gas. It was all about family and home, all about doing the right thing, no matter the sacrifice.

Just as our Lord did, Elise thought. She said a prayer for peace and hope, a prayer for thanksgiving and salvation.

*I will try, Lord,* she promised. *I will try to do what I know is right in my heart.*

Except, now that she'd discovered she wanted to be back here at *Belle Terre,* she'd also discovered that she'd fallen in love with a man she could never have. How did she reconcile the two decisions in her heart? How could she possibly be here every day, knowing Theo would be near?

I'll just have to remember my duty to *Grand-mère.*

That should keep her in check. That should occupy her thoughts and time. It would have to be enough.

With that declaration clanging in her mind, Elise smiled and took a deep breath of resolve. She would be all right.

He'd be all right. Theo stood in the yard of the great house, his gaze taking in the glow of candlelight and bonfire. *Belle Terre* shined like the great jewel of the bayou it had become. It was a beautiful house, but more so, it was a lovely home. He thanked God and Betty Jean Melancon for allowing him a glimpse of that kind of life, and in the same prayer he thanked God for his own family.

He thought back on last night when he'd taken his father to the cabin, thought of the tears of joy and pride in his papa's eyes. His *maman* had clapped her hands in praise, while his entire slew of brothers and sisters, cousins and kin had applauded his efforts. They had an old-fashioned *perlot* right there on the bayou. They'd eaten the rice and chicken concoction with cornbread and sausage, they'd laughed and shared tall tales and opened modest but precious Christmas treasures. His papa had read the Cajun version of the night before Christmas, always a favorite among his younger nieces and nephews. And then, his *maman* had asked Theo to read the second chapter of Luke—the story of the birth of Jesus Christ.

And Theo had understood things at last.

I belong here, he thought now. But he didn't belong in that mansion. I belong on the bayou with my family. No sense in hoping for dreams that couldn't come true. No sense in wishing for something he couldn't have. He'd just have to let Elise go back to her way of life and he'd continue to fight for his own.

"I'll will try to do right by You, Lord," he promised. "I will try to be a good man."

With that resolution, he headed up to the big house, not to gloat and celebrate, but to lay his heart bare.

He was going to tell Elise the truth.

# CHAPTER ELEVEN

She glanced up as he entered the parlor. Theo Galliano looked every bit the gentleman in his gray wool suit, crisp white shirt and red patterned tie, with his hair shiny and combed, and a soft smile of resolve and restraint on his face. Elise smiled at him, her heart bursting like a tree ornament that had fallen and shattered.

He saw her the minute he entered the parlor. Elise Melancon looked every bit the lady her *grand-mère* had taught her to be. She was wearing a green velvet sleeveless dress that favored a wide cummerbund nipped at her waist and a flowing full skirt that accented her pretty shape. She had on the pearls he'd become so familiar with. She sent him a smile full of hope and determination.

Theo hesitated as everyone began to find their seats. This was the moment he'd both anticipated and dreaded.

"Theo, where is Maggie?" Betty Jean called down the table. "We don't want to start without her."

Theo cleared his throat and sent up a prayer for

courage. "Maggie won't be coming, Mrs. Melancon. She sends her regrets."

"Oh, my."

He couldn't be sure, but he thought Miss Betty Jean was actually relieved. So was he. But he'd be even more relieved when he'd had his say and was out of here.

"I need to tell y'all something," he said, waiting as everyone got seated.

"You don't need to make a toast," Cissie said, rolling her eyes at this obvious breach of etiquette.

"It's no toast, I guarantee," Theo told her, his voice sounding decidedly more Cajun than cultured, and sounding far more calm than he actually felt. "It's a confession."

He centered his gaze on Elise. "May I?"

"Go ahead, Theo," Betty Jean said, almost as if she were cheering him on.

He stood at the end of the table, his eyes on Elise. "You know that Maggie and I broke up over two weeks ago. I believe the only reason she wanted to come here tonight, really, was so she could see this great house and tell everyone she'd been here. Or at least that's what she told me last time we talked."

There was an audible gasp among the adults and a rushed whispering among the curious children scattered at various tables throughout the room and adjoining kitchen.

"What do you mean?" Elise asked, rising up out of her chair. "I thought—"

"I know what you thought," Theo said, his heart thrashing with all the force of a mad alligator. "You thought helping me would bring Maggie back. I thought that, too, at first. But I've come to see I no longer love Maggie."

"You let me think that I was doing all of this for Maggie, for you and Maggie," Elise said, the tone of her voice showing her hurt and confusion, and maybe a trace of hope.

"*Oui,* I wanted to tease you a bit," Theo said, letting the hurtful look she threw him settle like a much-deserved slap on his face. "And then, I stopped wanting to tease you. I only wanted to impress *you,* Elise. Only you."

"Oh, good grief," Cissie said, her hands slapping on the table, the lacy cuffs of her white silk blouse fluttering. "This is ridiculous. And totally unacceptable."

"Let the man talk," Betty Jean said, holding up a hand for all to remain quiet.

Cissie sputtered and spewed, but she shut up.

"I only wanted to be with you," Theo admitted, the relief of it lightening his burden as he held Elise's gaze. "I like being around you."

"That is nonsense," Cissie shouted, looking toward her husband for support. "Darling, tell him it's nonsense."

"Let the man speak," Quincy responded, a curious light in his eyes as he watched his daughter.

"I find that…I find that I love you," Theo said, wondering where his plan for a fast exit had gone wrong. "I find that I fell in love with you, Elise. But I know that you can never return that love. I know that we aren't right for each other, at all—"

"You're as right as rain," Betty Jean said, her sharp gaze moving from her granddaughter to Theo.

*"Grand-mère!"* Elise said, looking in shock at Betty Jean. "You said you hired me for the job because I always run men off. You said there would be no chance that I'd fall for Theo."

"So I was wrong," her grandmother said with a dainty shrug. "It happens."

The expression on Elise's face changed so quickly, it reminded Theo of shadows moving across the swamp. She went from shocked and confused to understanding and amazed, all with the blinking of her beautiful eyes. *"Grand-mère?"*

"Yes, Boo?"

"Did you set me up?"

"Yes, darling, I surely did."

Cissie stood up. "What in the world are you talking about?"

Betty Jean stood, too, holding her water glass up in a salute. "A fine plan it was, too, if I do say so myself."

"What is going on?" Cissie said again, her voicing shrilling with each word.

"Our daughter is in love," Elise's father told his stunned wife, a knowing grin splitting his face.

"That's impossible," Cissie said, throwing her linen napkin down in a huff. "That just can't be. Elise, tell your father this is just plan silly."

Elise wasn't listening to her mother.

But Cissie saw very clearly what everyone else in the room had already figured out. "Oh, my," she said, plopping back down to stare at her plate. "Oh, my. It's just not possible."

Theo's eyes never left Elise's face, even though there seemed to be a flutter of activity all around them. He watched as she glanced first at her grandmother, then her mother, then finally back at him. "It's very possible, Mother. I am in love. I'm in love with Theo."

"No, you are not," Cissie said, her words bordering on hysteria.

"Yes, she is," Betty Jean said, grinning from ear to ear. "Let's eat."

Reginald appeared out of nowhere, a wide, joyful grin on his aged face. "We have a feast. I think I've outdone myself this time. Hope everyone's hungry."

"I couldn't possibly eat a bite," Cissie said. But when her husband gave a slight inclination of his head, she sat up in her chair. "Pass the rolls."

"We need to say grace," Betty Jean said, tears forming in her eyes as she looked from Elise standing at one end of the table to Theo at the other end. "We have so much to be thankful for. Such a joyous holiday."

As everyone settled down and closed their eyes, Elise motioned to Theo. He hurriedly followed her out into the hallway and watched as she grabbed a black velvet wrapper from a nearby hall tree. Together, they rushed out the front doors, the frigid night hitting them full force.

He caught up with her underneath a granddaddy live oak, tugging at her wrap until he had her turned and into his arms. "I do love you," he said, his words echoing out into the starlit night.

She gave him that famous pout. "Is that why you kept quiet about everything?"

"No, I kept quiet because I'm a bad, bad boy who wanted to irritate a good girl."

"It worked."

"Think we could make it work for the next fifty years or so?"

She leaned her head against the wool of his jacket. "I had decided to let you go."

"Funny, I'd decided the very same thing about you."

"We're supposed to be all wrong for each other."

"I know. That's what I keep telling myself."

She looked back up at him, then, her pout turning into a smile. "*Mamere* tricked both of us."

"That she surely did. What a smart woman."

"She's always been so wise."

"*Oui,* too smart for the likes of me."

"What are we going to do?"

"Well, since we so rudely skipped out on the blessing, I'd say first we send up a prayer."

She smiled at that. "Thank You, Lord, for allowing me to find this man."

"Amen, and ditto for me with this woman."

"What now?"

He held her close then pulled her wrap around her shivering body. "We are going to do the right thing, *chère.* We are going to spend the rest of our lives together, here on this bayou, in a home we'll build together. We're going to try and salvage what is left of this land. And our children will have a solid heritage."

"Children?"

"*Oui,* how many do you want?"

"Enough to run Melancon Oil and Gas, of course."

He turned serious then. "Do you believe we can make this work—I mean me and you—and your mother, and my family living off the land, and your family living in this big, old house?"

"I believe we can do anything as long as we trust in God and listen to my *grand-mère*."

"I can live with that."

"Me, too."

He leaned close, nuzzling at her pearl earrings. "What would a gentleman do in this situation, *chère?*"

She reached a hand up to touch his face. "Oh, you mean in a situation where he withheld the truth, teased his manners coach, disrupted a dinner party, caused a girl's mother to practically swoon, and made the whole family sit up and take notice?"

"Something like that?"

"He'd sneak his future wife out underneath a great oak tree and kiss her silly."

Theo laughed and swung her around in his arms. "Then you can consider me a gentleman. Your Cajun gentleman."

And with that, he kissed the woman he loved.

While the Christmas bonfire burned brightly beneath a perfect bayou moon.

\* \* \* \* \*

## DISCUSSION QUESTIONS

### 'Twas the Week Before Christmas

1. Why did Elise feel obligated to come home for Christmas? Do you believe family traditions are important and should be honored?

2. Do you believe people from two different worlds can live happily with each other? Why was it so important to Betty Jean that Elise get to know Theo?

3. What did Elise learn about family and commitment from Theo? How did his family mirror her own, even though they were worlds apart?

4. Did this story help you to realize that we stereotype some people? How did Betty Jean help Theo to make his dreams come true? What lessons did they both learn from this experience?

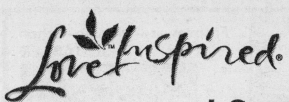

# A SEASON FOR GRACE

### BY
# LINDA GOODNIGHT

## THE BROTHERS' BOND

**Separated as children...
reunited as men.**

Police officer and former
foster child Collin Grace
wasn't fond of social
workers, even pretty ones
like Mia Carano. But Mia
knew he was the perfect
mentor for a runaway in
her care—and she wouldn't
stop until she unearthed
the caring man under
Collin's gruff exterior.

*Available December 2006,
wherever you buy books.*

**Steeple
Hill** ®

**www.SteepleHill.com**

# REQUEST YOUR FREE BOOKS!

## 2 FREE INSPIRATIONAL NOVELS
## PLUS 2
## FREE
## MYSTERY GIFTS

*Love Inspired®*

**YES!** Please send me 2 FREE Love Inspired® novels and my 2 FREE mystery gifts. After receiving them, if I don't wish to receive any more books, I can return the shipping statement marked "cancel." If I don't cancel, I will receive 4 brand-new novels every month and be billed just $3.99 per book in the U.S., or $4.74 per book in Canada, plus 25¢ shipping and handling per book and applicable taxes, if any*. That's a savings of at least 20% off the cover price! I understand that accepting the 2 free books and gifts places me under no obligation to buy anything. I can always return a shipment and cancel at any time. Even if I never buy another book from Steeple Hill, the two free books and gifts are mine to keep forever.

113 IDN EF26  313 IDN EF27

| | | |
|---|---|---|
| Name | (PLEASE PRINT) | |
| Address | | Apt. |
| City | State/Prov. | Zip/Postal Code |

Signature (if under 18, a parent or guardian must sign)

### Order online at www.LoveInspiredBooks.com

### Or mail to Steeple Hill Reader Service™:

**IN U.S.A.**
P.O. Box 1867
Buffalo, NY
14240-1867

**IN CANADA**
P.O. Box 609
Fort Erie, Ontario
L2A 5X3

Not valid to current Love Inspired subscribers.

### Want to try two free books from another series?
### Call 1-800-873-8635 or visit www.morefreebooks.com

* Terms and prices subject to change without notice. NY residents add applicable sales tax. Canadian residents will be charged applicable provincial taxes and GST. This offer is limited to one order per household. All orders subject to approval. Credit or debit balances in a customer's account(s) may be offset by any other outstanding balance owed by or to the customer. Please allow 4 to 6 weeks for delivery.

LIREG06